Saint's Prayer

More Romance from Phase Publishing

Also by
Grace Donovan

SAINT'S RIDE

Coming Soon

SAINT'S FOLLY

by
Rebecca Connolly

AN ARRANGEMENT OF SORTS
THE LADY AND THE GENT
THE MERRY LIVES OF SPINSTERS

by
Emily Daniels

DEVLIN'S DAUGHTER
LUCIA'S LAMENT
A SONG FOR A SOLDIER

Saint's Prayer

THE SAINTS OF LAREDO

BOOK TWO

GRACE DONOVAN

Phase Publishing, LLC
Seattle

If you purchased this book without a cover, you should be aware that this book is stolen property. It was reported as "unsold and destroyed" to the publisher, and neither the author nor the publisher has received any payment for this "stripped" book.

Text copyright © 2025 by Phase Publishing, LLC
Cover art copyright © 2025 by Phase Publishing, LLC

Cover design by Christopher Bailey

All rights reserved. Published by Phase Publishing, LLC. No part of this book may be reproduced or transmitted in any form, or by any means, electronic or mechanical, including photocopying or recording or by any information storage and retrieval system, without written permission from the publisher.

Phase Publishing, LLC first paperback edition
February 2025

ISBN 978-1-952103-77-3
Library of Congress Control Number: 2025931534
Cataloging-in-Publication Data on file.

Acknowledgments

This book is dedicated to all those striving to make a better life for themselves and the ones they love. You are not your past.

And, always, to my love.
More than a Saint, you're an Angel.

Prologue

GRANADA, KANSAS
1881

Reverend Thomas Jarrett, as he was known here in Granada, stood at his lectern in front of an empty chapel. Sunlight streamed in through the high windows on the eastern side of the church.

They weren't stained glass like one might see in the bigger city churches, but the framing had some lead work that added elegance to the simple arches.

The warm light reflected comfortably off the carefully polished pews and the well-maintained floors, giving the whole church a peaceful, almost celestial glow. He took great pride in the condition in which he kept the church. It wasn't large enough to require anyone else working here, so Thomas, the good reverend, handled all the custodial and landscaping work himself.

"The Bible is a tool," he said to the empty room. "A guide, to lead us on the path to God. We all start from different points, and so our paths are different, even though we all share a common destination. We all have challenges on our individual road. Some paths seem easy on the surface but can mask deep troubles…" he trailed off as his own thoughts drifted to the surface.

His own path had been troubled indeed. No one here in Granada knew about his past, and he preferred that it stay that way. The good men and women of this gentle town were unlikely to follow a man of God who'd once been a soldier for the devil.

He suspected the sheriff might have a notion about him, but the lawman had never said anything, so he couldn't know for sure. Not that the sheriff had ever been anything but warm and welcoming to him. But the name of Thomas Jarrett had been well known only a handful of years back, when he'd been young and dangerous.

It was still well known in certain circles, and more than likely would be for many years to come. In the darkest corners of the West, Thomas Jarrett was still a legend. Or so Jack Hannity, his old friend and brother in the Saints of Laredo, had told him a few months back.

Jack had come through in a rush with a bounty; a pretty but feisty little spitfire who had shaken the hard bounty hunter's world to the core. They'd come back a few weeks later, asking Thomas if he'd perform their wedding.

He hadn't been surprised. He'd seen the way they looked at each other, and that wedding had been an inevitability, whatever the two might have said or thought at the time.

There was love there. The real kind, that brought souls together in a way that those who didn't know God had a hard time understanding.

Jack Hannity didn't know God, or didn't stand much for talking about Him at any rate, but once that love had really hit him, he knew. Thomas smiled softly as he thought of his old friend.

Like himself, Jack was a good man who'd walked a rough road. In the end, in this life or the next, everyone gets what they deserve. And Jack deserved to be happy.

"Woolgathering, Reverend Jarrett?" came a creaking, slightly warbling voice he knew and loved.

His absent smile brightened into focus as his gaze turned down to the lovely old woman who stood at the side door.

Widow Riley was the kind of older woman who made it plain that she'd spent far more time in her long life smiling than anything else. Her multitude of wrinkles all curved upward, and even when she wasn't smiling, she seemed to be.

Her husband, Ben, had passed on many years before, long before Thomas had come to Granada, but he doubted even in her mourning that she'd given way to hopelessness.

Thomas had warned more than a few people not to let that fool them, though. The old bird was tough as ten-penny nails, and could give as good as she got, should one foolishly decide to take a shot at her.

She'd taken Thomas under her wing, almost like an adoptive mother, and helped him get settled when he'd first come to Granada. Of course, her bringing him cookies, much like the ones she now held on a plate in her deceptively delicate-looking hands, did a lot to win his affections.

"Mrs. Riley, are you trying to fatten me up? You brought me a whole plate of those wonderful oatmeal cookies not six days ago," he said with a wry grin as he stepped down from the dais and approached her.

"Now don't you get all shy on me now, reverend," she grinned. "You ain't never turned down a plate o' my cookies, and I sure as shoot ain't gonna let you start now! Besides, rats got into my cellar again and chewed through one of my bags of flour. Those rotten little vermin ain't getting my second bag! I had to use it, so I thought I'd whip up a batch of shortbread biscuits."

"Did you use the whole bag?" he asked, eyeing the tin plate of cookies. It didn't look like nearly a whole bag of flour's worth of shortbread.

"You bet yer last ducket I did!" she said with a laugh. "Those blasted rodents ain't getting' my flour! Made so many my counters are full of 'em! I'm using every plate I got to hand them out. I already gave a plate to everyone between my farm and here."

"Well, let me get a new plate to put these on, Mrs. Riley," he told her with a laugh. He graciously accepted the offered plate with one hand and gave her shoulder an affectionate squeeze.

"Oh, don't you worry none about that, reverend."

"It's no trouble," he assured her as he headed for the door to the rectory. "You've got to have something to eat on, assuming you haven't given away the rest of your food, too. Would you like some tea?"

"No thank you, dear. I'd better get to gettin'. Eight more plates to hand out, you know! One to the new family, as well. Did y' hear?"

"No ma'am, I haven't heard about anyone moving into town."

"Not right into town proper, mind," she replied, "they bought the old Kimber place."

"That so?" Thomas asked, surprised.

The Kimber farm had been vacant for near on a year now, ever since the Kimber family had moved up north to take over Mr. Kimber's uncle's place. The old fields had run fair wild since then. Good land though, and Thomas knew a few good hands could turn it around quickly, especially if they started right away.

"Sure enough. Word is, they got a few young rascals to feed. Well, that's no never-mind today. I'd best be off. If I don't hurry, I won't make it home by sundown, and then you'll be having to come rescue me from the coyotes!" she exclaimed as she flung one arm up in the air dramatically.

Reverend Jarrett laughed.

"You mean rescuing the coyotes from you, don't you?" he replied with a wink. "All right then, I'll come by on Monday and take a look at that cellar. We'll see if we can't keep those rats out for good." He turned and moved back to her.

"Sweet of you," she replied with her typical amused smile, as if she constantly saw a joke that nobody else got. "You can bring the plate back then, if you like." She reached out and patted his hand.

Her touch was gentle, and her hands looked fragile, but he felt the strength in them. She'd been running that farm by herself for years, though her son came by to help from time to time. This remarkable woman had never shied away from hard work. It didn't seem to be wearing her down, though. For all he knew, she'd live to be a hundred years old. Assuming she wasn't already, he amended.

Thomas prayed she would, if only to provide him with those frequent and charming smiles, pleasant and funny conversation, and random plates of her delicious cookies. Purely selfish, he knew, but her continued presence couldn't help but bring more light to the world on the whole, so he could somewhat justify his selfishness.

"It's a deal, Mrs. Riley. You take care, and I'll see you at service tomorrow."

She waved over one shoulder as she walked to

the door. She wasn't a fast walker anymore, but her steps were still strong and determined.

"Bring a gun!" she called back over her shoulder. "Blast those confounded little…" she trailed off, muttering curses about the rats. Thomas grinned and shook his head.

"I don't own a gun, Mrs. Riley!" he called out as she walked out the door. It closed behind her, and he shook his head again. "God bless," he added to the closed door.

It never ceased to amaze him that someone so full of fire and with a razor's edge could be so soft and sweet. It just went to show, he thought, that tough and kind were not mutually exclusive.

He absently took a bite of a shortbread cookie. He let out a soft, involuntary moan of enjoyment as he looked down at the cookie in his hand.

The woman was a marvel.

Turning to the rectory, he moved through the other side door out of the chapel and entered what amounted to his sitting room. A few more steps and he was in his small kitchen. He quickly re-plated the cookies and turned to the small wash basin to give Mrs. Riley's plate a quick rinse.

New residents of Granada, he considered. Granada was a small town, and everyone was quite close here. He hoped the new family would fit in well. While they were on the outskirts, they were still close enough that the town proper would see them often enough.

SAINT'S PRAYER

He spoke a quick prayer for the newcomers as he washed the plate, intending a more thorough prayer for them with the congregation tomorrow. Well, hopefully they were churchgoers, he thought.

The church could always use a few more friendly faces in the pews.

Chapter One

Sunday morning was as bright and filled with sun as the day before had been. Thomas had awakened comfortably, with the peace of a man who knows that all is as it should be in the world. That and the knowledge that there were still a few more shortbread cookies on the counter.

Even a beautifully sunny day like this one couldn't help but be improved by one or two of those.

By the time he'd finished preparing for morning services, the cookies were long gone, having neatly closed a good breakfast of fried eggs and buttered bread. The woman really was going to make him fat, he thought with a chuckle.

He stood at the door of the church, welcoming each member of his congregation as they entered. Thomas kept an eye out, though, for the new family.

"Good morning, Mr. Howard, Mrs. Howard," he said, shaking their hands as they passed with their own greetings. "Doc Williams, good to see you!" he said as the town doctor passed into the church with a smile and a handshake. A tug on his coat caused Thomas to look down.

"Good morning, Reverend Jarrett," came a sweet, soft, shy voice.

The face that met his eyes as he looked down was every bit as sweet, soft, and shy as her voice had been.

"Well, if it isn't my favorite young dancer," he said with a soft smile, crouching down to her level. "Good morning to you, as well, Miss Annie."

The little blonde girl, her hair in a neat braid down her back and her cream-colored dress freshly washed, blushed and looked down. Her eyes looked back up at him from under her long lashes. She was an adorable child and would grow to be a real beauty, he knew.

"My mommy said it was all right if I invited you for dinner on Tuesday. Will you come? Please?" she asked shyly.

He smiled broadly. It had been apparent from his very first sermon that Annie had been quite taken with him. It was charming and more than a touch flattering.

Thomas glanced up to see her parents standing a few feet behind her. It was uncharacteristically brave of Annie to step up and speak to anyone without her parents right at hand, and rare even then. She had clearly mustered every ounce of her six years of courage to invite him.

"Well, it's been quite some time since such a

lovely young lady invited me for dinner. I'd be positively delighted, Miss Annie. You can tell your mother I'd be happy to bring something along to go with the meal and to just let me know what time to show up."

Annie's eyes lit up at his agreement, and she looked fully up at him, smile bright and perfect. Anyone who ever doubted the existence of God, he thought, need only look into the eyes of a child as happy as Annie was at that moment. In those eyes was all the proof he'd ever need of a truly benevolent creator.

She spun about and raced back to tell her parents the good news. Annie's father, Sam Waterston, smiled at him and gave him a nod of thanks. Reverend Jarrett returned both in kind.

As he stood, turning back to the line of people entering the church, he realized he'd missed several people. It happened sometimes, and Annie's invitation had been well worth it, but he tried hard to greet everyone. It made everything a bit more personal.

When the last of his flock had entered, he stepped inside, leaving the doors open to the gentle breeze and fresh air. It would be a real sin, he thought, to leave the Lord's creation locked outside on a day like this.

He walked to the podium and stepped up. Looking down at the crowd, he immediately focused on a line of unfamiliar faces. They must have slipped by while he was talking to Annie, he thought.

They were anything but what he'd expected. A strong working man, his woman, and a couple of children would have made sense. He'd been told it was a family with a few children.

Instead, what he saw as his eyes ran the length of the pew was a delicate, pretty woman in a city dress, though not a rich one, five children ranging in age from twelve on down, and a second woman holding an infant.

The woman with the infant looked unhappy about something, and she looked decidedly out of place in the otherwise typical country dress she wore. It fit her well enough, but it just seemed not quite right on her. He couldn't quite put his finger on it, but there was something about her that tugged at his memories.

What he knew for certain about her, however, was that she was striking. She wouldn't have been called beautiful by everyone, but her features struck an unexpectedly warm chord within him that he felt resonate clear through him. In that moment, he would have called her beautiful and meant it without a wisp of guile.

He frowned slightly as he tried to process the unexpected development. The stunning woman with the infant frowned boldly back at him, her deep, dark eyes seeming to bore into him. They carried a weight of guarded disapproval that set him near on his heels.

Thomas couldn't for the life of him imagine what he'd done to offend the woman. She did look offended, though. Not highly, but noticeably, as if his mere existence was something she found mildly distasteful.

He glanced back down at his notes, trying to refocus. He took a deep breath, whispered a quick prayer, and began his sermon.

In seconds, the woman's eyes had left him, and instead focused on keeping the infant in her arms calm, and helping the other woman keep the five older children quiet and calm. They didn't seem naturally prone to that state, though. Not that quiet and calm was the default state for most children, he freely admitted.

The children were fairly well behaved, though, and while they squirmed throughout the sermon, they were relatively quiet and were not disruptive. The baby didn't cry once.

Thomas did notice that when the congregation prayed, the woman with the infant didn't close her eyes at all and seemed to be ignoring the prayer entirely. She did the same when the congregation sang.

He couldn't seem to stop staring, though she'd pointedly not looked his way once after her first disapproving frown his way.

How he managed to finish his sermon was beyond him. Something about her continued to tug at his mind, and his past. She was familiar, without being familiar at all. He didn't know her from Eve, but there was something about her he recognized. He just couldn't figure it out, though he sure tried.

"But for the grace of God," he muttered under his breath as he stepped down from the podium. How he'd made it through with his mind so distracted, he had no idea.

The congregation stood and began moving for the door. To his surprise, the two women and the flock of children moved toward him. Newcomers often stopped to meet their new pastor, but with the disapproving air the woman with the infant had given the whole service, he had expected the whole family to slip quickly and quietly out the door.

"Good afternoon," he said with a smile as they approached. "I'm Reverend Jarrett."

The woman with the infant stood half a step behind the other, who was the one to address him in return. She didn't seem to be doing so out of any shyness or reticence, though. Her entire bearing was one of pointed disinterest.

The other woman's smile was warm and open, and set him far more at ease than the unhappy woman did.

"Good afternoon, reverend," she said. "I'm Josie Briggs, and this is my sister, Rue Lewis."

She held one hand out to shake his, her other hand holding the hand of one of the younger boys, who looked up at him with interest, but no shyness.

Thomas shook her hand and smiled with a nod to the other woman, Rue, who still held the infant and showed no signs of offering a hand to him. She nodded back at him but looked impatient.

Her eyes were sharp and blue, such a dark shade as to be nearly gray. Her dark brown hair was pulled back along the sides of her head but flowed openly down her back in gentle curls.

"A pleasure, ma'am, ma'am," he said to each of them. "Welcome to Granada."

"Thank you," Josie replied. "Well, we just wanted to come introduce ourselves, and thank you for the lovely sermon. You're a bit more… well, let's just say that we're not accustomed to a sermon without a bit of yelling for punctuation."

Thomas laughed out loud. He couldn't help it. Rue looked at him, a faintly surprised look on her face at his laughter.

"I'm not much for the fire and brimstone speeches, Mrs. Briggs. My pa always used to tell me you catch more flies with honey than vinegar," he told them, "and I've always found that to be true. Besides, God is about love, isn't He?"

Rue's expression turned slightly considering, but she looked away the instant he glanced in her direction.

"True enough, reverend," Josie replied with a pleased smile.

"I do hope you'll pardon my forwardness, ma'am," Thomas said, "but may I ask where Mr.

Briggs might be?" He looked pointedly at the children, then at Rue, and back to Josie.

"My husband passed away nigh on six months ago, Reverend Jarrett. My sister came out to help me with the little ones and to help me get the farm started."

Ah, he thought, so the children belonged to Josie. For some reason he didn't want to dwell on, he felt slightly reassured by that.

"Mighty kind of you, ma'am," he said to Rue, who nodded her acknowledgement again, but didn't speak. To Josie, he continued, "I heard you bought the old Kimber farm. Good land out there. Just needs a little love, and it'll be producing some strong crops by summer. It's just the two of you working the land, then?"

"Three," the eldest boy, about eleven years old, spoke up, a defiant look in his eyes.

"Four," said the next oldest boy of about eight, who squared up and matched his older brother's strong gaze. The older boy put a hand on his brother's shoulder and nodded once firmly. Thomas couldn't help but smile.

In a flash, he'd assessed both lads in a manner he'd learned a long time ago for sizing up a potential fighter. These boys were definitely fighters. Maybe not with fists, but there was no doubt they had the grit they'd need to fight through the upcoming winter and get those fields producing.

"Well, in that case, you folks should do all

right," Thomas said to the lad directly. "A couple of strong women working the land could manage to get by, but a couple of strong young men like yourselves will make short work of things." The boys both relaxed somewhat, the younger one even offering a smile.

Since they were the men of the house, and clearly wanted to be taken as such, Thomas held a hand out toward first the older, then the younger boy.

"I'm Reverend Jarrett."

"Marshall," the older boy replied as he shook Thomas's hand with a surprising grip. They were dressed like city boys, but those hands weren't afraid of some hard work, Thomas instantly knew. No farm boy callouses, but a firm, bold grip.

"Robbie," said the younger, a bit of shyness showing now that he wasn't immediately backed by his older brother. His grip was firm as well, though.

"Pleasure, gentlemen. Listen close now," he said, glancing around like he was about to impart a secret. They both instinctively leaned slightly forward. "Those fields you've got are fine quality. The soil is good and strong, but you'll need to break through that tough topsoil to get to the good earth below. That land lay fallow all last season, so it's well rested and ready for a strong crop. Just be sure to give it a good turn before planting, get that rich, dark earth up topside again.

"Now," he continued, "I know you'll have to

make it the next six months on your own before you'll have anything usable off those fields, what with the season turning. If you or your mother or aunt need anything in the meantime, don't you hesitate to give me or any of your neighbors a shout. There's a lot of good folks in this town, and we believe in helping each other out. But you do right by that land, and she'll take good care of the lot of you once she's producing. You hear?"

The boys had listened closely and attentively, nodding periodically. As he finished, Marshall gave a firm nod.

"Thank you, reverend, we'll do just that."

"Good man," he answered with a smile. "Now, would you care to introduce me to the rest of these fine folk?" he added that last to Robbie, hoping to pull him a little out of his shyness.

"Well, sir, this here's my sister Georgia," the lad started, hesitating only a moment before pointing to the girl slightly older than he was, perhaps ten years old. "This one is Lucy," he continued, indicating a bright-eyed, six-year-old girl. "Then that one there's Mark," he finished, pointing at the younger boy, perhaps three, holding his mother's hand.

"And the little one?" Thomas asked, nodding a smiling greeting to each of the others in turn before indicating the infant held by Rue, who was watching him curiously again.

"That there is Thomas," Robbie said.

The boy stood a little taller and spoke a little

stronger than he had only moments ago, having been put in charge of something for a change.

"Thomas?" Thomas asked, letting a touch of pleasant surprise show on his face. "Well, what a coincidence. Thomas is my first name, too," he told Robbie with a wink.

Robbie grinned.

"It truly is a pleasure to meet all of you," he went on, "and I do hope you'll let me know if you need anything. Anything at all. A lot of people think that as a preacher, my job is just to stand up there and yammer on all day, but really that's just a small part. My job is to help the people in my community in whatever way they need. Be that helping birth a foal, tending someone who's sick, or even helping Mrs. Riley eat all those cookies she made." Thomas grinned as he said that last, and the older kids all perked up.

"Those shortbread cookies?" Georgia asked as she toyed with a curl at the side of her head.

Her own hair was styled in much the way her aunt's was, golden curls flowing freely and surprisingly long down her back. Thomas nodded his confirmation.

"She brought us a whole batch yesterday! They sure were good!" she exclaimed.

"It's not usually the preacher's job to confess," Thomas said conspiratorially, "but I feel obliged to confess that I ate a whole plate myself. If she brings me many more cookies, I'm gonna need bigger pants."

He puffed up his cheeks and stuck out his belly, which he rubbed dramatically. The kids giggled, their mother laughed, and he noticed out of the corner of his eye that even Rue broke a hint of a smile.

"Well, reverend, we'd best be getting on home," Josie said with a smile. "Thank you again for the lovely sermon. Would you like to come by for dinner on Tuesday?"

"That's awful kind of you, Mrs. Briggs," Thomas replied, "but I'm afraid I have already been invited to dinner that evening by the lovely Miss Annie." He gestured to Annie and her family as they headed for the door, having just finished a chat with the Tuckers.

Annie noticed and waved shyly. He smiled and waved in return. As he looked back, he noticed Rue's slight smile had grown a fraction, and her considering look was even more focused.

"Well, how about Friday?" Josie asked.

"Friday would be wonderful, Mrs. Briggs. I'll bring along some of my famous biscuits and homemade raspberry jam, if that's all right." He noticed the kids' eyes light up.

"That would be wonderful, Reverend Jarrett," Josie said. "We'll see you on Friday at six o'clock sharp." He nodded, and the family began to move away.

Rue held back a moment, still studying

Thomas. After another moment of assessment, she nodded to him once.

"Reverend," she said by way of farewell and turned, following her sister, nieces, and nephews.

Her voice was rich, deeper than he'd expected, and had a huskiness to it that sent a warm tingle up his spine. Again, something nagged at his memories, but he couldn't quite place it.

He promptly tossed out his first assessment that most men wouldn't quite call her beautiful. More than a minute in her presence and he had a hard time seeing how any man wouldn't be drawn to her like a moth to a flame.

There was a hardness to her, though. An edge that her sister didn't share. A sort of guarded caution, with a worldliness that her sister also lacked. It spoke well of her that she'd moved in with her sister to help care for the children when Mr. Briggs had passed, but that woman had some history, he knew. Not that he was in a position to judge. Not by a long shot.

He realized, as Rue cast one more glance back at him before vanishing out the door, that he'd been staring. With a quickly muttered prayer, he turned away and headed back to his office.

Chapter Two

"You sure weren't very friendly," Josie said to her sister, sitting beside her in the carriage.

"I wasn't rude," Rue said sharply in return. She knew her stony silence could easily have been seen that way, though.

"You weren't friendly," Josie repeated with a scowl. They sat in the back with the littler kids, Marshall and Robbie on the front bench as Marshall handled the reins.

"Churches and I ain't got a lot to be friendly about," Rue replied with a scowl. Josie sighed.

"It won't hurt you to attend services with us once a week."

"I'm not so sure," Rue muttered as she handed the small, wooden horse to baby Thomas.

His chubby little fingers grabbed the horse eagerly, and he gurgled his delight. Rue couldn't help but smile. Her little nephew had that effect on her. He was so full of innocence and delight in the world. Rue hadn't seen either in a very long time.

"Oh, come on, the reverend seems nice

enough," Josie said.

Rue glanced up at her. Nice wasn't the word she would have used. Sure, he was polite and friendly, but there was something there that her sweet, sheltered sister wouldn't have seen. The good reverend was a bit of a puzzle, in point of fact.

She'd seen enough cruel and harsh men in her life to know the man in the preacher's collar had some darkness in him. Not cruelty, no, but there was iron there. It confused her, though, because while the trace of darkness was definite, there was no denying that when he smiled and spoke to the children, the light in his eyes was every bit as real and undeniable.

When he laughed as he joked with them, the darkness deep down in his eyes almost totally disappeared. And those eyes… Rue forced down the sudden surge of warmth in her middle. She'd never seen eyes like that in a man.

They looked like they had once been blue but had faded in the harsh sun of the West to a smoky, steely gray. They held the unforgiving strength of steel too, but they showed a lot more warmth than one would expect. They weren't cold at all.

When she'd gotten her first look at him, she'd felt a flutter she hadn't felt in more years than she cared to admit. He was handsome, but she'd seen a lot of handsome men in her day. That strong jaw, aquiline nose, shadowed brow, and striking eyes meant nothing. The fluttery feeling had gone away almost instantly, until she'd stood close enough to him to see those eyes. Maybe those eyes did mean something.

Rue prided herself on her ability to read people. It had come in handy, letting her know who was dangerous and who was harmless. A useful skill in her former line of work. She couldn't get a firm read on the reverend, though. He was either a very dangerous man hiding beneath the guise of a good preacher, or a very good man with a terrible past. She couldn't quite figure which.

"Rue?" Josie's voice cut through her musings. Rue instinctively knew it wasn't the first time her sister had said her name. "Good gracious, Rue, one mention of the reverend, and you go all quiet and thoughtful-like. If I didn't know better, I'd say he struck a nerve with you."

Rue rolled her eyes.

"Please. I was just contemplating the agony of another fifteen years going to church with you every week. Preachers are all alike. 'Praise Jesus, say your prayers, give me your money... for the poor, of course'," she mocked. Josie laughed.

"He never once said any of those things," Josie protested as she played with Lucy.

"Just wait, it's coming," Rue said wryly. Josie laughed again.

"I can't wrangle all six of these wildcats without you, Rue. Don't make me try it in church, of all places!"

"I'm not going to abandon you, Josie, you know that," Rue said softly. Josie's eyes and tone softened, as well.

"I know, Rue, I know. I can't tell you how much it means that you've left everything and come all the way out to…"

"You've said that already. At least fifty times in the last week," Rue interrupted with a roll of her eyes. "Lord knows we don't need to go re-hashing it every time you get sentimental. You're my sister. You'd have done the same for me."

"I certainly would, but it still means a lot that you did," Josie said, "especially what with…" Josie trailed off and glanced away. After a moment, she looked back and continued. "And who knows? This is a new town, with new faces, and a whole passel of new people to meet. Nobody here knows a thing about you. It's a real fresh start. We might find you a man of your own out here."

Rue scoffed.

"Oh, honey, I've had enough men to last a lifetime. No, thank you, that door closed a long time ago."

"You never know," Josie replied with a noncommittal shrug. Rue rolled her eyes.

"Believe me, I know," she muttered.

The wagon began to slow, and the two women looked up at Marshall. They were nowhere near home yet.

"Ma, look," Marshall said, nodding his head to

the side.

A sheriff on a horse stood to one side of the road, watching them expectantly as they approached. Marshall stopped the carriage. The sheriff trotted up alongside the rear of the carriage to speak to them.

"Afternoon, folks," he said, with a tip of his hat.

"Afternoon, sheriff," replied Josie.

Rue kept her mouth shut. She didn't get on with lawmen any better than she did preachers, and for a lot of the same reasons.

"You the new folks up at the Kimber place?" he asked.

"Yes, sir," replied Josie. "Just moved in from Topeka."

"Welcome to Granada," he replied with another tip of his hat. "Listen, I don't want to take up much of your time, I just wanted to give you folks a bit of a warning. I was just out at the Dalton place, and he says he's seen sign of natives on the outskirts of his land. His farm is right next to yours, so chances are, they've been around your land, too."

Josie paled slightly, looking over at Rue. Josie had read a book once about the tribes of the West and had since developed an irrational fear of them.

Rue knew better. It was a little concerning that they were roaming the edges of cultivated land, though. Tribes in these parts usually kept their distance from the white men, Rue knew. If they were around, they wanted something.

"Goodness, sheriff, are we in danger?" Josie asked, hand to her chest.

"Don't you worry none, Ma. I'll protect us," Marshall said firmly.

"Yeah," Robbie agreed, as he always did when Marshall spoke.

"No, ma'am, I don't reckon there's any real danger," the sheriff reassured them. "Mostly the natives around here just want to keep to themselves and be left in peace. We don't bother them, they don't bother us. I just thought you'd want to know, so you could be sure to take some basic precautions."

"Thank you, Sheriff…" Josie said, leaving the last word hanging as she waited for his name.

"Rawlins, ma'am. Sheriff Rawlins. If you folks need anything, don't you hesitate to say so. Good folks around here."

"So we've heard," Josie said with a smile.

So far, Mrs. Riley, Reverend Jarrett, and now Sheriff Rawlins had all said exactly the same thing.

Rue tried hard not to roll her eyes. In her experience, good folks were the rare kind. Her sister was one of the very few people in this world she ranked among those precious few. And her kids.

They really were great kids, though Rue wasn't generally much for kids herself.

She honestly didn't think she was capable of them, if it came to that. Lord knew if she had been, she'd have been with child a long time ago, precautions or no.

But these kids really were good ones.

"Well folks, I'd best be moving along. I want to go speak with the O'Leary's on your western side, see if they've seen any signs on their lands, too. Can't be too cautious," he said. With another tip of his hat, he trotted off on his dappled mare.

"Indians," Josie said with a shudder. "Do you suppose…"

"No," Rue immediately countered. "No, I don't suppose. The sheriff would know if the tribes around here were dangerous, and he didn't seem too troubled by it. We'll be just fine. We'll just take a few precautions, like keeping the rifles at hand. And maybe getting a dog," Rue added.

Instantly, all the kids in the carriage whipped around to look at her excitedly. Except maybe little Thomas, who was happily trying to fit the entire wooden horse into his mouth at once, with a surprising degree of success.

"A dog?" they shouted in unison. Josie glowered at her.

"Really, Rue? Thanks for that. Now they won't talk about anything else for days."

Rue shrugged, unconcerned by her sister's ire.

"It's a good idea, Josie. A good dog can solve a lot of problems on a farm. There's a reason people joke about country boys and their dogs."

"Can we get a dog, Mama? Can we really?"

Robbie asked, the pleading in his voice impressively heartbreaking.

"No!" Josie snapped, still glaring at Rue.

The kids were crushed, and Josie clearly blamed Rue for it. Rue didn't feel bad, though. Maybe they'd help her convince Josie to get one. A guard dog really wasn't a bad idea.

Maybe they could ask Reverend Jarrett where to get one, she mused before catching herself. She shook her head to rid it of the thought. Why him? Why not the sheriff? Or Mrs. Riley? Or their neighbors, the Daltons or the O'Learys? Why not absolutely anyone in town except the reverend?

Because whether she wanted to admit it or not, she wanted to see the reverend again. Just to solve that puzzle, of course. The enigma that man presented promised the most excitement she was likely to get for a long time in a town like this. That's all it was.

The thought of his smile brought that fluttery feeling back.

Get a hold of yourself, she thought angrily. Not only did she not want anything quite so much as she didn't want a man in her life, he was a preacher! A worse match she couldn't possibly imagine, even if he weren't forbidden from marriage to begin with.

This wide-open air was already getting into her head, she decided. Thinking all manner of foolishness.

Little Thomas squirmed in her arms and made

a bit of a fuss. Rue looked down and bounced him gently, playing with his fingers as she murmured to him. He calmed quickly and smiled up at her.

They were much better off with a dog than a man, she thought. Men were dirty, controlling, demanding, aggressive, and for some reason she'd never quite gotten her head around, seemed to view women as second-class citizens. Dogs were just dirty.

Although, Reverend Jarrett had seemed awfully clean, her traitorous mind pointed out. She barely restrained an irritated grunt at her own thoughts.

He was a preacher and was married to God, or some such nonsense. And she really, truly, sincerely didn't want a man in her life. At all. Marshall was as close to a man as she cared to have in her world at the moment, and his voice hadn't even started to crack yet.

As if her thinking his name had called him, the boy glanced back at her from the driver's seat. He gave her a smile, which she returned. Now that boy would become a fine man, she thought. Josie's husband had been a good man, too, she knew.

There were good ones out there, if she were forced to admit it. But they were unquestionably the exception, and she didn't care to waste her time looking through the overwhelming majority to find a gem. Especially right now, when she and Josie had so much work ahead of them getting this farm running.

Neither of them had ever worked land before. The boys hadn't, either. Josie had brought a dozen books on it, though, and they were sure they could manage. Maybe the advice of someone local who knew the land, like Reverend Jarrett, would be helpful.

This time she did groan in annoyance. Her thoughts simply refused to stay away from him. That puzzle he presented was obviously taking control of her mind. She wouldn't rest until she figured it out. She would…

"What?" Josie asked, having heard the groan. Rue looked up at her sister's curious expression.

"Nothing," she lied.

"Liar," Josie said with a grin. Rue's own smile slipped out at her sister's directness.

"Just thinking about how much work we have to do," Rue said, which was mostly true, "and that maybe we should talk to our neighbors and get some advice."

"That's a good idea, Rue," Josie agreed. "Let's go over tomorrow and meet the neighbors. If anyone can help us figure out this farming thing, it's the farmers next door, right?"

"Right," Rue nodded. "Let's do that."

That was that, she decided. There was no need to ask the reverend for his advice. Or for anything. Ever.

Chapter Three

"That's true enough, reverend," Mr. Dalton was saying. He leaned against the waist-high, white picket fence surrounding the churchyard while Thomas leaned on the hoe he'd been using in the garden. "Them Injuns can be a right mess o' trouble," the man said.

"Some can, that's true," Thomas agreed, "but not most of them. No more or less than white folks."

"Sorry, reverend, but maybe your church schooling didn't teach you much about the ways of the world," Mr. Dalton said. Thomas almost laughed at that. "Them Injuns is savages! Any one of 'em will just as soon scalp ya as look at ya."

Thomas seriously considered telling Mr. Dalton about Storm-Chaser, the tracker that had long been his friend. Storm-Chaser had been the one to lead Jack Hannity out of the old gang and helped form the Saints of Laredo, along with Thomas himself, Lucky, Kid Grady, and Santiago. A better man didn't exist in this world, of that

Thomas was certain.

Telling Mr. Dalton that would require some context and raise questions, though. Thomas wasn't prepared to let that cat out of the bag, yet. If ever.

He'd be run straight out of this fine town if anyone ever learned their preacher was a former killer of the finest caliber, and at one point was widely acknowledged as the best gunfighter west of the Mississippi. And probably east of it, too, though he'd never been out that way to find out.

Thomas was a fine example of repentance and the healing power of God, but the good people of Granada probably wouldn't let him get far enough to explain that much.

"Now don't go judging people, Mr. Dalton. Especially people you ain't even met," Thomas told him. "'Judge not, that ye be not judged'," he quoted.

Mr. Dalton had the grace to appear slightly embarrassed, which looked a little funny on a man his size. It wouldn't be at all a stretch to mistake him in a dark forest for an angry bear.

"You're right, preacher, o' course. I just heard tell of some mighty scary stories of them Injuns."

"I understand, Mr. Dalton. Fear is a powerful thing. But if a dog bites you and you learn to fear dogs, it in no way means that every dog will bite. Most of them are just friendly as can be. People and dogs are much the same. Some are friendly, some are loving, some are fearfully aggressive, and some are just downright mean. Some of the aggressive and mean ones will turn loving and friendly if you show them a little of the same. Some won't. The Tsawi are practically our neighbors here and are probably the tribe who are scouting the outlying farms. I don't know why they're coming so close, though. If they keep coming around, I'll go out and speak to them."

"You'll what?" Mr. Dalton asked, astonished.

"No harm in talking," Thomas answered.

"There is if they scalp you!" the big man replied in horror. Thomas chuckled.

"The Tsawi don't scalp, Mr. Dalton. They don't kill people for no reason, either. If they're around, they probably need something. They might just be trying to think of the best way to ask."

"It just don't make me feel any better, knowing they're wanderin' about my lands at night."

"I can understand that, Mr. Dalton. You just let me know if you're still finding fresh tracks in a day or two, all right? I'll head on out and see if we can't find out what they want."

"Well, if you insist, reverend, but I…" Mr. Dalton kept talking, but something had pulled Thomas's attention elsewhere.

A carriage was rolling down the road toward the center of town. He immediately recognized the family riding in it. They recognized him, as well, though that was not a difficult task due to his distinctive garb. Several of the kids smiled and waved happily.

Thomas smiled and waved back, but his eyes

were already looking for someone else. Sitting in the back, half buried under the littler kids, was Rue. Josie, who also smiled and waved, sat across from her.

Mr. Dalton had noticed his gaze, and both men tipped their hats at the ladies as they approached.

Rue looked up as she noticed the children and her sister waving. Locking eyes with him, he couldn't read her expression. It was very carefully controlled. Josie said something to Marshall, who guided their horse and carriage alongside the fence. Rue now looked slightly annoyed.

Thomas couldn't have said just why, but her annoyance amused him.

"Good morning, ladies," Mr. Dalton said, tipping his hat again.

"Did ya hear, reverend?" Robbie said excitedly. "We've got Indians on our land!"

"Yours, too?" Thomas asked in surprise, glancing at Mr. Dalton. Mr. Dalton gave him a slightly smug look, which made Thomas smile.

"Yes, sir," Marshall replied. "We went out looking for signs and found this!" The boy held up the tip from a broken arrow. Now Thomas frowned.

"May I see it?" he asked, holding out a hand. Marshall handed it to him.

"Lots of horse tracks and footprints, too," Georgia added. "Maybe a hundred!"

"There weren't that many," Marshall said with a scowl. "There's maybe only ten of them," he added to Thomas. "Fifteen at the most." Georgia made a face at her brother.

If they were natives, that meant there probably were a hundred, he thought. He didn't say so, though. The Tsawi were good at masking their numbers. And at hiding their trails, which made the broken arrowhead and numerous clear hoof and footprints even more unusual.

He looked at the well-made arrowhead closely. It was a flint arrowhead, typical of the Tsawi, and the sinew cording was typical as well. There was no blood on it. The break just behind the arrowhead was clean, like it had been stepped on or snapped by hand. It certainly wasn't broken by being fired at anything.

The edge of the arrowhead was sharp and unmarred, too. It didn't look like it had ever been fired at all.

But if it hadn't been fired, and there would have been no need to fire an arrow out there, why was it even out of the brave's quiver? Leaving it broken on the ground was very unlike a scouting party.

"Where's the shaft?" Thomas asked Marshall.

"The shaft, sir?" he asked, confused. Thomas held up the arrowhead.

"The tail end of this arrow. If the head is here, where's the shaft?"

"I don't know, sir, we only found that."

Which meant it was possible someone had carried the shaft away, leaving the arrowhead. That made no sense at all. It was unlikely that it had broken when someone stepped on it. They'd not have picked up one piece and not the other. The heads were harder to make anyway, so it was odd that if only one piece had been carried off, it was the shaft.

He glanced up to find Rue looking at him with that same puzzled, considering look, like she was trying to deconstruct him. That warm tingle ran up his spine again. Her gaze suddenly made him feel very exposed. He looked down, hiding her from view with the brim of his black hat.

"Something very strange here," he muttered, looking again at the arrowhead. "Which side of your land?" he asked the family. Josie answered.

"Up on the north."

"Same at my farm," Mr. Dalton said. "The Briggses and I had a chat about them savages the other day. I told 'em to get on out and check for signs. Looks like they found 'em."

"It's not normal behavior for the Tsawi at all," he said, half to himself.

"Maybe it ain't the Ta-sa-we," Mr. Dalton said, butchering the pronunciation.

"Maybe not," Thomas agreed.

If it were, it would be very unusual for a number of reasons. But if it was another tribe, why were they in Tsawi territory? Why scouting out Granada's outlying farms? Why leaving such obvious evidence? It made no sense.

"We're taking that to the sheriff," Georgia said matter-of-factly.

"And going shopping," added Lucy from the other side of Rue.

Thomas looked up and smiled at the girl, showing her that she'd been heard and acknowledged. Instantly, he wished he hadn't. His look immediately brought Rue directly into his line of sight. He felt his eyes pulled to her, despite his best efforts.

"That sounds like a marvelous idea on both counts," he told the young girl, forcing his eyes back to the child. She grinned at him. He turned to look back at Marshall and Robbie but caught Josie's eye, as well.

"Listen, boys," he told them seriously, "the Tsawi are peaceful folk. I'd bet my own Bible they don't mean you any harm. I don't yet know why they're about, but I suspect they need something, and are just trying to figure out who's best to ask.

"Do me a favor, and if you see one on your land, don't shoot at him. They may not mean any harm, but if you start shooting at them, they may shoot back, and things will get mighty ugly for everyone around here. If you see one on your land, you come find me or the sheriff to go talk to them. Trust me, the Tsawi aren't here looking for trouble. It's not their way."

"I trust you, reverend," Marshall said, but he looked troubled.

"Me too," Robbie agreed.

"I'm glad to hear it," he told them. "You're fine young men, and if you keep a good head about you out on that farm, you'll be all right. If you're still finding new signs in a couple of days, come let me know. I already told Mr. Dalton I'd go have a word with the Tsawi if they're still around by mid-week."

Robbie's eyes went wide.

"You're going to go talk to the Indians?" Robbie asked, voice filled with awe. Thomas smiled at him in amusement.

"They're good folk. Just trying to live their lives in peace, like we all are. If they're still around in a few days, I'll go have a word with them and see what we can do to help them out."

His eyes slid back to Rue of their own accord. She was staring at him. Her expression had shifted again and was once more unreadable. His inability to get a fix on her was driving him crazy. He resisted the urge to give an annoyed growl. Barely.

"Well, I'll sure be keeping a weather eye out," grumbled Mr. Dalton.

"You do that," Thomas agreed. "Just don't go shooting at shadows. Or any native scouts, unless they fire first."

"All right, preacher," Mr. Dalton agreed reluctantly.

"When you folks speak to the sheriff," Thomas said to Josie, "just tell him the facts, like you told me. He knows the Tsawi, as well. He'll get you sorted."

"All right, Reverend Jarrett. Thank you very much," she replied with a smile.

"Are you settling in all right?" he asked, shifting topics. The discussion of the Tsawi scouts had him a little on edge. He knew the tribe very well. None of this made any sense, and he needed time to think about it.

"We sure are, thank you," Josie said.

"Is there anything I can bring for you? Help you with?" he asked. Even to his own ears, it sounded slightly eager. He forced himself not to glance at Rue. Mentally, he berated himself.

"No, we're just fine without you," Rue replied, a little sharply. Josie looked over at her sister, a curious expression of amusement on her face.

"No offense intended, ma'am," Thomas quickly replied. "It ain't easy settling into a new place, but I'm sure you folks are managing just fine. I only ask because it's my job to help lighten the load of the people here, spiritually, emotionally, and sometimes physically. Just let me know if an extra set of hands, or a borrowed tool or two might make things a bit easier on you."

"We sure will, reverend," Josie said, still smirking at Rue.

"Well, we'd best be along," Rue said pointedly to her sister. Thomas nodded and tipped his hat. Mr. Dalton tipped his, as well.

"Pleasure speaking with you folks again,"

Thomas replied. "I look forward to Friday."

"Us too," Marshall said with a smile.

"Yeah," agreed Robbie.

Marshall clucked his tongue and gave the reins a gentle flick. The horse began an easy walk as Marshall steered them back toward town.

Rue watched him for several more seconds before turning deliberately away and staring off into the distance as they rode out of sight. She was a perplexing mystery, he thought.

He didn't think he'd be nearly as fascinated by the puzzle she presented if there wasn't something so familiar about her. He still couldn't place it, but the way she carried herself was distinctive. Thomas just wasn't sure of what.

"Quite a family," Mr. Dalton said suddenly, interrupting his thoughts.

"They are that," Thomas agreed. He glanced over, but Mr. Dalton was dusting off his hat.

"Well, preacher, I'd best be off m'self. If you get the chance, head on out by my place. I know where some o' them tracks are, and you can have a look, since you seem to know those Injuns so darned well." Mr. Dalton looked up at him, a thoughtful look on his weathered face.

Thomas could have groaned. He'd let too much out of the bag, and now Mr. Dalton was curious. Thomas would never forgive himself if his own carelessness opened up his secrets to the town. He loved this town, and all the people in it. Being chased out of it over his past sins would be a crueler fate than he could imagine, though he couldn't say it wouldn't be well deserved.

Thomas tipped his hat to Mr. Dalton and watched as the man wandered off down the road. Thomas sighed.

Things sure seemed to get complicated fast, he thought.

There really wasn't any reason he could think of for the Tsawi to be nosing around. Let alone for them to be leaving such obvious traces that a city boy with no experience could spot them.

The broken, unfired arrowhead without a shaft, the obvious foot and hoofprints, even the numbers implied made no sense. The Tsawi scouting parties were small, usually only a handful of braves, and it would take a tracker of Storm-Chaser's skill to spot any traces of them.

All the evidence pointed to carelessness that was completely alien to the Tsawi. But he couldn't deny the Tsawi design of the arrowhead and cording. Maybe he needed to head out and talk to their chief now.

His own history had long taught him that carelessness from a warrior was a sign of desperation. If the Tsawi were getting desperate, he couldn't be sure it wouldn't get violent soon. He just couldn't figure out why they'd get that desperate without coming to ask for help. They knew he was here in town, and their chief knew him more than well enough to know he'd help them any way he could, if asked.

It was a mystery every bit as confusing as Rue Lewis.

The depth and hardness in her eyes spoke of a long, difficult history. Not as difficult as his own, maybe, but that was all relative. She'd clearly suffered, and become stronger for it, as he had. But suffered from what?

Her sister seemed as innocent and sheltered as most city women, though she seemed perfectly friendly and quite open to the idea of the work that lay ahead of her, caring for that land and her family.

Whatever had happened, it had happened only to Rue. She seemed puzzled by him, too, he realized. Perhaps she, too, could see some of the edge on his soul etched by years of pain and suffering, some received, some given. The scarred recognized the scarred. Perhaps she was having trouble reconciling that with the white collar he wore. She wouldn't be the only one.

The real trouble was that her sharp, worldly eyes might root out the truth of him faster than Mr. Dalton's innocent curiosity ever could. Dalton could be redirected. He strongly suspected that Rue Lewis would not be so easily derailed.

She wasn't just a mystery, she was a problem.

Chapter Four

Shopping was normally one of Rue's favorite activities; not that she'd ever had a lot of money to indulge with. The house had kept most of her earnings.

This time, they had some money and a lot of equipment, tools, food, and clothing to buy. She should have been deeply engaged with her sister and her nieces, who all enjoyed shopping as much as Rue herself did.

Instead, she found herself holding Georgia's hand and only half-listening as the girl rambled on about what kind of dresses she wanted while they finished buying tools for the farm. Her thoughts were elsewhere. On a particularly intriguing, darkly handsome priest.

She'd known hundreds of men in her day, though most only for one night, but none had pulled at her thoughts the way the steely-eyed reverend seemed to.

Rue had argued with herself constantly since his sermon that it was simply because of the peculiar puzzle he presented, a man with a warm gaze that hid a hard interior.

Only she didn't think that was entirely right, either. That was part of the puzzle. She could see the hardness in his eyes. She could see the darkness lurking there. When he looked at her, she could see a man others would fear hiding behind a warm gaze. But when he smiled, that frightening element disappeared. And nobody else seemed to see the deeper darkness at all.

He was nothing but polite and friendly, his gaze and smile warm and open. But he was hiding something, some part of himself secured under lock and key.

And the way he looked at her… well, that had certainly been a new experience for her, as well. She'd been ogled by enough men to last a lifetime, had even encouraged it to bring in new customers, and she'd known plenty of men who wouldn't give her a second glance, as well.

Reverend Jarrett looked at her. Not at her body, not at her clothing, but at her. Those piercing eyes of his seemed to look right into the deepest parts of her soul. When that man looked at someone, he really saw them, on a level far deeper than most. She knew that without a doubt.

He seemed to be trying to understand her, much as she was with him. A couple of folks with shadowed pasts, trying to make a living as something they weren't. They were quite a pair, she thought with a smile.

She almost stumbled a step at that. Not that they were a pair, she quickly amended to herself. That wasn't how she'd meant it at all.

And she didn't really know that's what he was, after all. He might well be a dangerous criminal hiding from the law here. The warmth and openness could be faked. She knew that well enough and had been the victim of more than one friendly face in her early days away from home.

But Reverend Jarrett wasn't like that, she felt. She didn't know why she felt that about him, but she did. The warmth was real. But so was the edge she could see behind it.

Not that it mattered. She really needed to stop dwelling on him. Reverend Jarrett was completely unavailable.

And why should she even care whether he was available? He was a priest, she didn't even know the man, and she didn't want or need a man in her life anyway! The entire idea was ridiculous.

But then why couldn't she stop thinking about him?

She sighed heavily in annoyance and winced when Georgia stopped and looked up at her, hurt.

"I'm sorry, honey," Rue told her niece. "That wasn't for you. Just trying to figure something out, and it's very frustrating."

Georgia eyed her accusingly for a long moment, then her expression softened.

"That's all right, Aunt Rue. I was just saying that the store probably won't have the color of dress that I really want, and…"

Rue did her best to focus on the girl's rambling about dresses, she truly did. She dearly loved the girl, but Georgia, when she was comfortable, chattered nonstop. Around strangers like Reverend Jarrett, she clammed up quickly, but it wouldn't take long for her to relax around the man and start talking his ear off, too.

He did seem to have a great way with children. He'd sure had no trouble getting Marshall and Robbie to warm to him. And the way he'd smiled and waved at the other little girl, Annie she thought he'd said, had been nothing short of charming.

That move alone had sent her…

Wait, she thought, how had he come up again? The confounded man simply wouldn't leave her alone!

They walked through the door of the general store, and Rue looked around. It was surprisingly well stocked, considering how small the town was. She knew they wouldn't find everything they needed here, but apparently more than she thought they would. And she was sure the shopkeeper could order anything for them that he didn't have on hand without too much trouble.

"Mornin', folks," said the kindly, portly man behind the counter.

She wasn't sure why, but it seemed an

unwritten rule that to own a general store, you had to be portly. She couldn't ever recall seeing a general store shopkeeper that wasn't.

"Good morning," she replied with a smile and a nod. Josie echoed her.

"Can I help you folks find something?" he asked.

"Oh, we've got a list here, sir," Josie said with a light laugh, moving his way. True to her word, she produced a carefully written list and handed it to him.

The shopkeeper looked it over thoughtfully, nodding now and then, and pointing at occasional items, though he seemed to be doing so just for himself, as he wasn't showing them the items he was pointing to.

"Well, I reckon we can get most of these here items off my shelves, but you've got a thing or two we'll need to order in from the city. Do ya need it all right away?"

"No, sir," Josie replied. "We didn't figure we'd get it all here today. You'll have more than we thought you would already, looks like. How long will it take to get the ordered items?"

"Oh, not more'n a week. Old Randall Evans makes the trip down to Topeka and back twice a month to pick things up for me. He's heading out tomorrow, as a matter of fact."

"That's wonderful, thank you!" Josie replied with a bright smile.

It was good news. Rue had been afraid they'd have to wait a month for some of the tools. She couldn't imagine many folks came out here to farm without so much as a hand spade to their name. They were starting from scratch in every way, and the sooner they could get that land worked, the more likely they were to beat out the first frost.

"If yer boys there want to help me start loading things onto the counter, we can make short work of this list, ladies," he said, coming out from behind the counter and dusting one hand on his apron, the other still holding the list.

"We can help, sir," Marshall replied.

"Yeah," agreed Robbie.

The trio wandered off down the aisle while Rue and the girls moved toward the front of the store to look at the hats in the front window. Josie stood by the counter, holding little Thomas in one arm and holding Mark's hand with her other.

Idly, Rue ran her fingers along the edge of a lovely, wide-brimmed white hat, with delicate purple flowering along the band. It was classier than anything she'd ever worn. It was nice enough for church, she thought. She'd need a good church dress to go with it. Purple would match the hat nicely. She wondered what the reverend's favorite color was.

She pulled her hand away from the hat like it had burned her. Good heavens, she thought, this is getting out of hand.

"Well that's the prettiest hat on the prettiest girl," a kindly voice said, thankfully interrupting her thoughts.

Rue turned to see Widow Riley entering the shop. She automatically smiled as she spotted the older woman. Rue had taken an instant liking to the woman and couldn't imagine that anyone wouldn't. There was a spark in her that was impossible not to be drawn to.

Widow Riley was talking to Lucy, who had put one of the hats on, though it was far too big for her, and had been posing in front of the full-length mirror next to the hat stand.

Lucy grinned and struck another dramatic pose. The Widow Riley clapped her hands once and beamed.

"Absolutely beautiful. The boys here in town had better watch out for you girls!"

Georgia giggled while Lucy made a disgusted face. Widow Riley chuckled.

"And how are you today, Miss Briggs?" she asked Rue. Rue nodded.

"Well enough, Mrs. Riley. Just getting our supplies for the season. Going to be a long winter until we get our first crop."

"Should be a mild winter, I think," Widow Riley replied.

"How can you tell?" Rue asked, curious.

"Oh, the smell of the air, the note of the birds' song, the way the squirrels are playing. You get to be my age, and the little things can tell you a lot about what's coming," the old woman replied. Rue couldn't help but shake her head in amazement as she smiled.

"That's remarkable, Mrs. Riley. Are you ever wrong about it?"

"Not in thirty years. Used to drive my Ben crazy. He never quite got the knack of it." Widow Riley laughed. "We used to place wagers on it. I'll tell you, girl, I got more new dresses that way…"

Rue laughed in kind.

"I'll have to get my dresses the old-fashioned way, I'm afraid," Rue replied.

"Oh, for now," Widow Riley said, with a glint in her eye. "More than one eligible bachelor 'round these parts. Won't be long before they come a'calling." Rue couldn't hide the grimace, though she tried. Rue could tell from the considering look that came to Widow Riley's face that she'd noticed it, though.

"I'm a bit off men at the moment, Mrs. Riley. Some bad experiences back in Topeka. Maybe someday," she conceded out loud. That'll be a cold day in hell, she thought in contrast.

"Sorry to hear that," Widow Riley said, patting Rue's arm in a comforting manner, though her eye was still filled with curiosity and a bit of a scheming glint. "Don't you worry none, ain't nobody here going to push you into anything. You'll get a few suitors, mark my words, but you shouldn't have much trouble begging off. Boys 'round here are taught to be respectful of women."

"That's a first," Rue said without thinking. Widow Riley gave her a wry smile.

"You really did get burned, didn't ya." It wasn't a question.

"In a way, ma'am. But I'm all right. Just need some time to get my family here settled before I can start thinking about me."

"You do that," came the reply, "but don't be surprised if God has other plans."

Rue almost sighed in annoyance at the mention of God. Before she could reply, though, Widow Riley continued.

"Speaking of God, have you met the good reverend?"

For the third time in as many minutes, Rue tried desperately to hide her reaction. More successfully, this time, she was pleased to note.

"We have, yes. Spoke to him after the sermon. He's coming over for dinner on Friday, in fact."

"That's wonderful, dear! He's a good man, that one. Don't get no finer. He's coming by my place later today to help me deal with them rats. You know, the ones that ate into my flour?"

"The reason you made those cookies," Rue added. Widow Riley grinned broadly. Rue was surprised to see a full set of surprisingly strong-looking teeth.

"Them's the ones. Anyway, he's coming by to

keep them out of my cellar, so I need to buy me some more flour. I'm plum out."

"I'm disappointed to hear that," Rue admitted.

"Hear which? That the reverend is coming, or that he's keeping the rats out?" Widow Riley asked with a merry twinkle in her eye.

Rue laughed lightly, though the image of the reverend with his shirtsleeves rolled up and working hard was one she couldn't completely push out of her mind.

"The rats. They sure did all of us a favor. Those cookies were absolutely divine."

Widow Riley laughed and patted her arm again.

"Don't you worry none, dear. Rats or no rats, there'll never be a shortage of cookies in this town. Not while I'm still on this side of the soil."

"I look forward to many, many more years of cookies, then," Rue replied.

"Your lips to God's ears, dear," Widow Riley replied, crossing herself with a grin. "But when it's my time, I'll go with no regrets. I look forward to seeing my Ben again. Nobody on this green earth more fun to tease than that man." Her tone was fond and wistful.

Rue felt a pang in her heart at the sound. This was a woman who had known true love, and the care of a genuinely good man. Part of her wanted nothing to do with men ever again, but try though she may, she couldn't fully deny that part of her ached for the kind of love the Widow Riley's voice held in that moment.

It wasn't the fairy tale, sugary, happily ever after kind of love. It was the kind of love that came from living, working, struggling, sharing together, day in and day out, hand in hand, for decades. It was the kind of love that was tempered and strengthened by the years of building a life for yourselves out of the very earth itself. The kind of love the stories should be written about. Cinderella, eat your heart out, she thought wryly.

"Mrs. Riley!" Marshall and Robbie called in greeting as they came around the corner of an aisle, each with their arms loaded with goods.

Like everyone else Rue could imagine, the boys had taken an instant liking to her. The cookies had been an easy in for these two, though, Rue admitted to herself with a grin.

"Howdy, boys!" she called with a wave. "You two fine gentlemen care to help an old woman out? I need two bags of flour carried out to my wagon, and I don't think I can manage all by my lonesome."

Rue doubted that a great deal. She was fairly sure this small, wiry, potent woman could have carried her own horse home, were it to go lame, but she wasn't going to point that thought out.

"Yes, ma'am," Marshall agreed with an easy smile, unloading his armful of supplies onto the counter before running back to grab a bag of flour. Robbie hurried to do the same.

"Mornin', Mrs. Riley," the shopkeeper said as

he, too, came around the corner. He was carrying several tools.

"Mornin', Jacob. How's yer wife doing? She feelin' better?" Widow Riley replied.

"Yes, ma'am, she sure is," he answered. "I'm fair certain those cookies worked better magic than Doc's medicine did." The pair laughed and Rue grinned.

The easy nature of the folks in this town was completely alien, and completely wonderful, to her. It was so different from the interactions of the folks in Kansas City. Everyone there was always in such a rush and were so short with one another. There was always someone nearby angry and yelling.

She hadn't heard anyone yell in anger in weeks, and she just now really recognized what a difference that absence made. She suddenly started to understand what everyone meant when they kept talking about the good folks around this town.

"Oh, I'm fair certain they didn't," Widow Riley replied, "but I'm sure glad she liked them. Can you put those two bags of flour on my tab?" she asked as the boys passed by her out the door, each carrying a large sack of flour.

"Sure thing, ma'am," he replied.

"Thank you, Jacob. You give my best to the missus."

"I will, thank you, Mrs. Riley." Jacob waved as the Widow Riley patted Rue's arm one more time and shuffled for the door.

Just before she made it outside, Widow Riley paused and looked back at Rue.

"Apple pie," she said.

"Pardon?" Rue asked, confused.

"For dinner on Friday," Widow Riley clarified. "Apple pie is the good reverend's favorite." The old woman winked and headed out the door.

Rue felt her cheeks flushing slightly. She couldn't remember the last time she'd blushed. Putting one hand up to her cheek in astonishment, she stared at the now empty doorway. How had she…

Oh, this wasn't good, she thought.

Not good at all.

Chapter Five

He didn't have to wait long after knocking. The door was opened almost frantically, young Annie standing behind it. She gave him a particularly charming smile that was a blend of shyness and eagerness.

"Evening, Reverend Jarrett," she said.

"Good evening, Miss Annie. You look particularly beautiful today," he replied with a smile.

He noticed she was wearing her yellow dress. It was the same one he'd told her at the town festival two months back was the prettiest dress he'd ever seen. Thomas didn't think it was a coincidence she wore it again today.

She beamed at him.

"For goodness' sakes, let the man in, Annabelle!" he heard her mother call from somewhere in the depths of the house. Annie blushed in embarrassment.

"Please, come in," the girl said, stepping aside.

"Thank you kindly," he replied, stepping inside.

Their home was neat and tidy, and while small,

wasn't cramped. The scent of roasting meat brought a soft grumble to his stomach. He smiled in anticipation and followed Annie toward the dining room after she closed the door behind him.

She practically skipped down the hall. Entering behind her, he smiled at her mother.

"Evening, Mrs. Waterston," he said.

He immediately noticed another man he didn't recognize sitting at the table. The other man stood but didn't immediately approach.

Mrs. Waterston stood at the wood-burning stove, stirring something in a pot. She looked back over her shoulder. Her blonde hair, identical to her daughter's, had been tied up in back of her head to keep it out of the way. She smiled at him.

"Good evening, reverend. We're so pleased you could come."

"I couldn't possibly have refused," he said with a laugh, winking at Annie, who blushed.

"Sam's out finishing up work in the field. This is his brother, John, visiting with us for a month on his way up north. John, this is Reverend Jarrett."

Thomas held out a hand. His quick eye had already assessed John Waterston, and determined he was a solid, dependable kind of man, like his brother. Not complex, but sturdy as the earth and just as reliable. John was the bigger of the two, broader in shoulder and brow, but had the same smile lines by his eyes.

"Pleasure to meet you, John," Thomas said.

John shook his hand with a grip like a vice. Thomas returned it in equal measure, causing a glint of surprise to appear in John's eye.

"Good to meet you, reverend," John replied.

"What's that?" Annie asked, pointing to the two bottles, one large, one small, held in Thomas's hand.

"Annie," her mother scolded.

"Sorry, Ma," Annie replied, looking down. Thomas laughed.

"It's quite all right, Mrs. Waterston. Nothing wrong at all with a bit of curiosity in a child." He turned back to Annie, who had looked back up at him. "This bottle," he indicated the larger one, "is wine for the adults. And this one," he indicated the smaller bottle, "is nothing other than root beer for my lovely young hostess."

Annie's eyes went wide. The stuff was hard to come by outside the city and was expensive even there. The slow, excited smile that spread across her face was completely worth it, he decided.

"That's awfully kind of you, reverend, you didn't need to do that," Mrs. Waterston said. "Please, have a seat."

"No trouble at all," he replied, setting the bottles on the table and sitting across from where Annie was sliding into a chair.

He meant it, too. Thomas had his own secret stash of the stuff. He would never have admitted this to anyone, but he preferred root beer to even the finest of wines.

"How long have you been reverend here?" John asked as Mrs. Waterston turned back to the stove.

"A couple of years," Thomas replied, "ever since Reverend Leonard passed away. Good town here. It was a real blessing being sent here myself, though it's my first official calling."

"Still pretty new to the game, then?" John asked. Thomas nodded.

"Relatively. It's a good town, though, and a real pleasure to be part of this community. There's some work involved, sure, but if you love what you do, it's hard to really call it work."

"That's true, that's true," John said musingly.

"So, you're on your way up north?" Thomas asked him.

"Yes, sir. I've got a claim on some land up in the Dakota territory. Going to establish a ranch."

"Rough country up that way. You're in for a hard winter."

"I know it," John replied. "I'll be up there before the first frost, get the lay of the land, and then winter in White River while I get established."

Thomas nodded and opened his mouth to reply, but the side door opened, and Sam Waterston walked in. Thomas stood with a smile.

"Evening, Mr. Waterston," Thomas said.

"Just Sam is fine, reverend," Sam replied, shaking his hand firmly. "Welcome."

"Thank you," Thomas replied. "You've got a beautiful home."

"Thank you. It's not much, but we love it."

"Love is everything, Sam. If you've got that, you've got all you need."

"Couldn't agree more," Sam replied, taking a seat at the table beside his brother. "You hear about the Indian attacks up by the O'Leary's?" he asked.

Thomas's blood went cold. Attacks? There was no reason for an attack, and it would be very unlike the Tsawi.

"No, I hadn't heard. Anyone hurt?" he asked. Sam shook his head.

"Not serious. Dennis got a bit of powder burn on his hand when his old rifle misfired, but none of their shots hit him."

"Was he able to recover any of the arrows?" Thomas asked.

"Not arrows, bullets," Sam clarified. Thomas's frown deepened.

"Bullets? The Tsawi almost never use guns. They believe killing with a gun is disrespectful to their enemy."

"And killing with an arrow ain't?" John scoffed.

"They believe when you take another life, your spirits connect in that instant," Thomas explained. "In that, they believe there is honor and nobility, and respect for your enemy. They don't feel that taking a man's life with a gun creates that same connection. It shows a disregard for the strength of your enemy's spirit. Killing someone with a gun is considered a grievous insult."

"Well, Dennis was mighty insulted, then. They were for sure trying to kill him, and they weren't shy about using guns," Sam said.

Thomas was more perplexed than ever. If the Tsawi were using guns, they would only be doing so if they felt their tribe had been dishonored and insulted to an extreme degree.

But more than that, if a hunting party of Tsawi had come through looking to kill Dennis O'Leary, Mr. O'Leary would be a corpse right now. But he hadn't even been wounded, which implied they were trying to scare him, not kill him. Which never had been a Tsawi tactic. None of it made any sense.

He would have to head out and speak to their chief sooner rather than later. Things were escalating too quickly.

"Boys, can we not discuss such unpleasantness at the table?" Mrs. Waterston asked, her tone chiding.

"Of course, ma'am, my apologies," Thomas replied.

"No trouble, I just don't want you scaring Annie."

Thomas looked at Annie, but she didn't look concerned. She was watching him with a shy look of adoration. He smiled at her, and she blushed.

"My apologies, Miss Annie. How has school been?"

Annie made a face. "I don't really like it, but it's all right, I suppose."

"Why don't you like it?" he asked. She shrugged.

"I'm not very good at arithmetic."

"Neither am I, I have to admit. But it's good to learn," he replied.

"I don't know why. I'll never use it," she said sullenly.

"Maybe not," he said noncommittally, "but you're learning how to learn. That'll help you learn things later that you will use all the time."

She considered this a moment, then nodded.

"I suppose you're right," she said thoughtfully. Thomas grinned.

"So, John, a month is a long time for a visit this close to the end of the season. Especially with you heading north," Thomas said, turning back to the men.

"Well, I don't know when I'll be back through these parts, and I wanted to spend some time with my brother. Besides, I was kind of hoping I might find me a wife while I'm here," John explained. Thomas nodded.

"Makes sense. If you're going to be up there on your own settling your claim, a good wife will be a godsend. There are a few eligible women in town."

"Widow Riley is single," Annie said with a mischievous giggle. Everyone but John laughed.

"Honey, I don't think Widow Riley is looking,"

Sam replied.

"Widow Riley?" John asked, curious.

"Lovely woman," Thomas explained. "And a hard worker."

"So, what's the catch?" John asked. Thomas chuckled.

"She's likely about old enough to be your grandmother," he answered. John laughed.

"Maybe not a great match, then. Any better ideas?"

"There's the eldest Marley girl," Sam said thoughtfully. "She's pretty enough, and not afraid of a little work."

"Jenny Holt is single, too," Mrs. Waterston replied. "She's a bit plain, but you'll forget all about that the moment you taste her strawberry tarts."

"Miss Gentry is available, but I'm not certain she's looking, either," Thomas added thoughtfully. Annie giggled.

"You can't marry Miss Gentry!" she protested in a tone that said clearly she felt she was stating the painfully obvious.

"And why not?" John asked with a playful huff.

"She's my teacher! That would be so peculiar!"

Thomas laughed along with John.

"Well," Thomas said with a sigh, "there goes that option."

"What about the new family?" Mrs. Waterston asked.

"The Briggses?" Sam asked, raising a brow.

"She's only recently widowed," he pointed out.

"No, not her, her sister. What's her name?" Mrs. Waterston asked.

"Rue," Thomas said without thinking. Too quickly, he realized as they all glanced his way. "Rue Lewis, I believe," he hedged, hoping to sidestep their sudden curiosity. It seemed to have worked, he observed with some relief. They paused, considering the suggestion.

"She's a handsome woman," Sam said with a nod.

Handsome was not the term Thomas would have used, but he supposed he could see its application here. It just seemed... inadequate.

"She's helping her widowed sister with those six children," Thomas said, hoping irrationally to derail the course of Rue's place in this conversation.

"Maybe I could bring her up after the winter," John mused. Thomas felt a surge of irritation.

"I don't think she'd be willing to leave her sister," he said. "She's only just moved all this way to help out with the kids after the loss of her sister's husband. I don't think it'd be right to take her away from them any time soon."

He realized it was quiet as they all looked at him. Had he said too much? The last thing he needed was anyone jumping to the conclusion that he was attracted to Rue. That was ridiculous anyway.

It was.

"Well, there's still Jenny. And Susan Marley,"

Sam said after a pause, looking back to his brother. "Either one of them would make a fine wife."

Thomas leaned back, oddly relieved that they seemed to have pulled Rue from the roster. The whole thing was absurd, he told himself. She seemed to have a powerful dislike for him anyway, and he wouldn't be looking for a wife himself, even if it weren't forbidden to his order. So why it mattered, he couldn't have said.

But it did.

Chapter Six

Rue heard the farmhouse door open seconds after the sound of a knock. Robbie must have already been in the front room, she thought as she rose from the back-room floor. Josie and Marshall were out behind the house, clearing weeds from the path to the well, so they likely wouldn't even have heard the knock.

She shuffled around the boxes she'd been helping to unpack and moved to the doorway. A short walk down the narrow hall, and she was in the front room.

At the door stood... she realized she'd never actually caught the shopkeeper's last name. Poor manners on her part, she thought in annoyance. She'd heard Mrs. Riley call the shopkeeper Jacob, but she didn't think she'd ever actually heard his last name.

His beefy arms were loaded with boxes and packages, items he'd said he'd bring around later, since he'd have to do a bit of digging to get them out of the storeroom.

They were mostly tools, things people around here probably didn't buy often, since most of the families in this kind of town probably still used their old grandfather's tools.

She was honestly impressed that the man had many of these items at all. He did have to order a few things in from the city, and they wouldn't be here until next week, but they had more than enough to get started.

"Ma'am," Jacob said, tipping his head, since his arms were too full to reach his hat. He smiled at her, then nodded to Robbie, who had gotten the door for him.

"Oh, please come in with those!" Rue said quickly. "You can just set them here, by the bookcase."

He did so and was followed almost immediately by another man.

Reverend Jarrett, she thought with an odd blend of excitement and exasperation.

The reverend nodded with a smile to Robbie as he passed him, his own arms carrying several long tools. When his eyes met hers, she saw a bit of a guarded look enter them, but it wasn't unpleasant. Just the kind of look one gave when you weren't quite sure if a dog would be friendly or bite your hand the moment you extended it.

That wariness satisfied her, for some reason.

"Howdy, ma'am," he said simply, giving her a nod as well.

"Ran into the reverend on the way out here, and he offered to help me unload the cart," Jacob said as he lowered his armload to the ground by the bookcase. "Well, I'll be," he said in wonder as he stood from depositing the packages on the ground. "Can't say as I've ever seen quite so many books in one place afore," he said, eyeing the bookshelf.

She was reluctant to admit that she hadn't, either, before moving in with her sister. Books weren't exactly cheap out here, but Josie's late husband, Mark, had been something of a collector.

There were at least four dozen books on the bookshelf. Although many of them were new ones on farming Josie had bought just before they came out this way.

"My late brother-in-law loved books," she explained. "And we picked up a few before coming out here, to help us learn the farming side of things."

"Sounds like a man I'd have gotten on well with," Reverend Jarrett said, setting down his own armload of tools and kneeling before the low, rickety bookshelf.

"Are you a reader, reverend?" she asked, a bit dryly.

"I dabble," he said with a smile cast up her way from his crouched position. "Not something I did much of in my youth, or any at all, beyond what I was forced to do for school. It's fascinating what interests a man can develop over time, though."

"I'll bet," she replied.

His expression shifted unexpectedly, a bit of a playful, challenging light coming into his eyes.

"The Bible must be riveting the twentieth time you read it," she said with a bit of a cutting note to her voice.

She wasn't quite sure why she felt the need to poke at him like that. She didn't really want to antagonize him. Quite the opposite. Which was precisely why she felt she had to.

"I recently finished a work by a gentleman named Fyodor Dostoevsky," he said, standing to look her in the eye, that playful glimmer still shining in his gray eyes. "The copy of *Crime and Punishment* that I have was translated into English from its original Russian, I don't speak a word of it, myself, so I'm sure it lost a touch of its elegance along the way, but it really was an interesting work. Some unique insights into human nature, I felt, though a bit heavy-handed in parts."

His expression still held that slight challenge, too, daring her to argue with him. She couldn't. She had no idea who Dostoevksy even was, let alone anything about *Crime and Punishment*. She'd been dying to dig into Mark's old books but hadn't yet had the time.

Rue hadn't had much opportunity to read in her adult life, but she had dearly enjoyed the opportunities she'd been given.

It was a complicated emotion that swept through her, surprised that he truly was a reader, impressed that he was reading such apparently sophisticated work, and annoyed that he'd called her bluff.

"I prefer Dickens, myself," she lied. His smile broadened.

"I'm quite glad to hear that, ma'am," he said. "I've been meaning to give Mr. Dickens a try but have never been sure where to start. Anything you'd care to recommend?"

"*A Tale of Two Cities*," she said at once.

She'd been wracking her mind to remember any of his titles, and that one had conveniently come to the front of her thoughts the moment he'd asked. Small miracles, she thought.

His expression turned approving and a little impressed. He hadn't expected her to have an answer, she realized with irritation.

"Thank you, Miss Briggs, I'll be sure to remember that next time I have the chance to get my hands on a new book."

"Well," she said, smoothing down the skirt of her dress, "is that all then, gentlemen?"

"No, ma'am," Reverend Jarrett told her. "At least one more load for the pair of us, if your man here will give us a hand," he said, indicating Robbie with a questioning look.

"Yes, sir," Robbie replied with a grin, just happy to have been called a man.

He was so sweet with the children, she thought. And that's plenty of that, she mentally berated herself.

"We'd best get it all brought in, then, Mr. Applebee," Reverend Jarrett said, "and let these fine folk get back to their day."

Applebee, she thought with pleasure. That was the shopkeeper's name! She made a mental note to remember it. It felt awkward thinking of him by his first name when she'd never even been formally introduced to the man.

The two men headed back outside with Robbie. They were back a minute later, each once more laden with goods.

They unloaded around the first piles and stood, regarding their work.

"That ought to about do it, I think," Mr. Applebee said. "Thank you, son, for the hand," he said to Robbie, who nodded. "I'd best be off." Mr. Applebee tipped his hat to her and nodded to Robbie. "Ma'am, son, you folks have a nice day."

Mr. Applebee turned and walked out. Reverend Jarrett didn't move to leave yet. Once more, her emotional response was a blend of excitement and irritation. And the former just fueled the latter.

"Reverend?" she asked impatiently.

"I won't keep you, Miss Briggs," he said, his rich, smooth baritone resonating somewhere in her chest, "I just wanted to ask if there was anything I could help you folks out with, while I'm here. I'm happy to help out anywhere I can."

"No, reverend, that's quite all right," she

replied sharply.

It really was very kind of him to offer, she thought, but the last thing she needed was him hanging about and causing that traitorous tug-of-war in her emotions.

"I don't mean to press," he said, clearly intending to press, but his expression had turned slightly abashed, which she found quite charming, "but if I don't find some excuse to stay away from the church house for a few hours this afternoon, Mrs. Rigby and Mrs. Taylor will pin me down for a deeper discussion of Revelations and Abraham. Mrs. Rigby's gotten it into her head that the end of times is upon us and has gotten Mrs. Taylor all riled up about it. Miss Briggs, I just don't think I can take that conversation today. Really, if you've got anything that needs doing, I don't mind. You'd be doing me a fine favor, and that's a fact."

She laughed, to her own surprise. The image he painted was too funny for her to resist. At her laugh, his smile broadened again, showing his clean, straight teeth.

Fine, she thought in a tone of annoyance, though she was feeling less of that by the minute already. He could help, but she'd set him to a chore outside the house and away from her.

"Well, all right, reverend, if you insist. There's weeds all around the well that need pulling."

It was a tedious chore and would be difficult work, she knew. The weeds by the well had grown particularly well in the absence of a caretaker for the farm. She was half-hoping he'd pass and head on out, but she knew he wouldn't. She already had him figured for an honorable man, or at least, pretending to be one, so after his offer to help, he wouldn't say no, regardless what horrible task she gave him. She had no doubt whatsoever that he'd have dug a new outhouse pit for them if she'd asked it of him.

Hmm, that had possibilities, she thought.

He spoke, interrupting the visual she'd begun of him digging and covered in sweat, blessedly just as the image had turned from something she intended to be funny and smugly satisfying into something satisfying for entirely different reasons.

"No trouble at all, Miss Briggs. I'll head right on out and take care of it." Reverend Jarrett tipped his hat her way. "Robbie," he said, shaking Robbie's hand again before heading back outside, closing the door behind him.

She took a deep breath and let it out slowly.

"You all right, Aunt Rue?" Georgia asked from the couch where she played with baby Thomas.

"Fine," she snapped, angry with herself far more than Georgia. She hadn't even noticed the girl was in here.

She turned and moved to storm back into the back room, and promptly tripped over a shovel.

Rue yelped as she reached out frantically to catch herself, but grabbed the handle of a second shovel instead, bringing the whole pile of tools over on top of her with a tremendous ruckus.

She had a half a breath to lie there and curse her stupidity before both the front and back doors burst open. Josie and Marshall rushed in from the back, and Reverend Jarrett from the front.

The front door was closer, so he reached her first.

Of course he did.

She wasn't even lucky enough for the fall to have killed her to spare her the embarrassment.

Chapter Seven

"Miss Briggs, are you all right?" Thomas immediately asked, concern filling him.

That crash had been something else, and he was afraid she'd hurt herself on either the tools or the floor. He immediately began carefully moving the tools from on top of and all around her.

"Yes, I'm quite all right, reverend. The only thing hurt is my pride."

"Good heavens, Rue!" Josie exclaimed.

"I said I'm fine, Josie," Rue said, her irritation evident in her voice.

The tools cleared, Thomas held a hand out to her, which she took with an expression that displayed all the reluctance in the world. He hoisted her carefully to her feet, other hand going around behind her back for support. He was watching closely to make sure she didn't favor a leg or something.

When she didn't, he let go of her hand and removed his other hand from around behind her. His eyes met hers again. She held his gaze a moment, then looked sharply away.

"You sure you're all right?" Josie asked.

"Yes," she grumbled, smoothing the front of her dress again.

"If you're sure, I'll head on back and start on the weeds by the well, then," he said, moving back to the door.

He glanced back her way before he closed it, not convinced she was fine, but she seemed none the worse for her tumble.

Moving around the back of the house, he spotted the well not far from the back door. The weeds were still rampant all through the yard, but the path to the well had been freshly cleared. Good work, too.

Thomas promptly pulled a pair of work gloves from his back pocket, something he'd brought in case he was able to convince Josie to let him help out a bit. He wasn't expecting to be greeted by Rue, though.

It bothered him that she was so insistent on disliking him. She had a real problem with the church and its priests, but why, he couldn't have said. All he knew was that he was determined on two points.

First, to convince her that the church, and this particular priest, truly meant her no harm and only wanted to help them get settled into town and their new farm.

And second, to try and figure her out. It still

nagged at him how familiar some of her mannerisms seemed, and it was driving him plum crazy that he couldn't figure it out.

He'd been working no more than five minutes when he heard the back door slam shut. He looked up, and to his surprise saw Rue walking toward him. She didn't look thrilled.

He straightened and regarded her.

"Something I can do for you, Miss Briggs?" he asked.

She stopped a few feet away and sighed, the sound one of frustration.

"Do you ever do anything besides offering to help people?" she asked.

"Not really," he admitted with a smile. "It's both my job and my pleasure."

She shook her head in resignation.

"Well, this is my job now. You're welcome to head on home," she told him. He frowned slightly.

"No thank you, ma'am. If it's all the same to you, I'll keep working," he answered.

She frowned in response. He noticed a small furrow between her brows. It appeared every time she frowned, he realized.

"Well, I've been told to do it, and I aim to. So kindly shift over and I'll join you, if you insist on keeping at it."

He did as he was told, sidling a quarter of the way around the stone-built well housing. He began pulling more weeds. They worked in silence for a few minutes before he dared speak again. But when he did, he intended to make it count.

"Miss Briggs, I want to make you a deal."

She straightened, expression surprised and eyes wary.

"I'm listening," she said, the words slow and cautious.

"I don't know what your history with the church is, but it's plain as day that you don't care much for it, or those who share its message."

"If you're going to ask why, I'll stop you right there, reverend."

"No, ma'am. It ain't none of my business," he quickly reassured her.

"All right, what then?"

"Whatever your history, someone in the church quite plainly did you wrong. For whatever it's worth, I'm deeply sorry, and even more deeply troubled to hear it. It ain't the way the church should be treating people."

She still eyed him warily, but not quite so much as before. He took a moment to steel himself. This next part was a risk. It would either set the first paving stone on the path to her shedding her universal dislike of priests and churches or would set her dislike to new levels.

"You and I are starting fresh here. There's no bad blood between you and I personally, it's just my office that troubles you. That much is clear. So, here's my offer. I won't preach to you. Not one word, besides what you'll hear in my sermons on Sunday, which will never be aimed anywhere but at the congregation as a whole. No preaching, ever."

Her gaze was steady, considering.

"And what price are you hoping to extract for this lofty concession?" she asked.

"Judge me for me," he said simply.

"Pardon?" she asked, clearly surprised.

"That disdain you've been tossing about any time I'm around? Just put it away long enough for me to show you whether or not I rightly deserve it."

Her expression was still guarded and considering, but her eyes rolled through a series of thoughts he could almost read like words on a page. He'd taken her completely off her guard, and she wasn't at all sure how to respond. Surprise, consideration, guilt, and shame all made their appearances in due turn.

He let her chew on what he'd said a long moment. Eventually, she sighed, and he saw a wall drop. Not all of them, not by any means, and not all the way, but it was a fine beginning.

"You're right, reverend. I owe you an apology. I haven't been fair to you. I'll try to do better, but please understand that I've spent a lot of years avoiding the church, and not for no reason. It'll take some time."

"That's all I'm asking, Miss Briggs. Just give me a little time. Not all priests are worthy of the calling. None of us are, in the purest sense, but some of them aren't holy men at all. I truly wish we all were, but that just ain't the way the world works. But maybe, just maybe, some of us try our very best."

Rue nodded, and he felt a weight lift from his shoulders. The idea that she'd hated him had weighed on him in ways he didn't quite understand. Her willingness to give him a fair shake took that weight away, and he felt lighter than he'd expected to.

Thomas gave her a smile, nodded, and went back to pulling weeds.

They worked in silence for several more minutes, Thomas casting surreptitious glances her way. She was a good worker, which didn't surprise him, though he couldn't have said why.

"Why become a priest?" she asked suddenly. He glanced up. She was watching him in a way that told him it wasn't the idle question it seemed.

"Pardon?" he said, though he'd heard her clearly.

He was hoping she'd elaborate her intentions a little. Luckily, she did.

"Well," she explained, "most priests join the order young. Almost born and raised, in a lot of cases. This is your first post and you've only been here a couple of years. You did something else before this, so it wasn't your first choice. So, why become a priest?"

Thomas hadn't told her this was his first post. He hadn't told her he'd only been here a couple years, either. She'd been asking about him. Something about that pleased him a great deal.

"Tried a few other things before joining the order, that's true," he answered slowly, puzzling out how to answer her question in a way that would be honest, tell her nothing, and still satisfy her question.

Her explanation had only reaffirmed what he'd already suspected. She was quite bright. And was also unfortunately inquisitive. It was a dangerous combination, but he didn't feel threatened by it in her case.

He should have, he knew. It wouldn't take a lot of digging to find out who he really was. Thomas wasn't even using a false name. He'd thought about it, but some sense of accountability in him refused to do so. If someone tracked him by his name, it wasn't as though he didn't deserve whatever came. And so, he'd left it in God's hands.

"Did some business with my brother for a few years, at first," he went on, "then left for another organization. Worked with them for a few years, too. In the end, neither really suited. They weren't making me the man I really wanted to be. So, I turned to the church, and here I am."

There. That was specific enough to satisfy most people, and vague enough to not actually tell her anything.

"What sort of work?" she asked curiously.

Blast, he thought. Too inquisitive by half.

"Acquisitions, mostly," he responded, trying

not to sound too pleased with his own quick, clever response.

She didn't look convinced but didn't press. Thank God.

"How about you?" he asked. Turnabout was fair play, after all. "What were you up to before your sister needed your help?"

"Now that, reverend, is none of your business," she replied tartly. He chuckled, and she looked up from the weeds once more, a slight scowl on her face. "What?"

"Sensitive subject, I see," he replied. "I won't probe any deeper there, I apologize."

Her glare held strong for a moment, then she gave a soft huff.

"I worked in the city, assisting my boss's clients in bringing their unique problems to a satisfactory conclusion," she said.

He could have laughed. She was good at this game, and he was enjoying playing it with her. Instead, he gave her a considering look.

"What kind of problems?"

"Our clients had a variety of issues we were able to help them with, all of which are confidential."

"Fair enough. Difficult work?" he asked.

To his surprise, she actually seemed to give this legitimate consideration. After a moment, she shook her head.

"Not too demanding, if I'm being honest. More

emotionally wearing than anything else."

"Do you wish you could go back to it?" he asked.

"No," she said without hesitation. "Even if it weren't for Josie needing me, I wouldn't go back to it if I had a choice. How about you? Do you regret leaving your last few jobs for the church?"

It was his turn to give serious consideration to the question.

"In a way. I miss working with my brother, but not the work itself. Not at all. As for the other organization…" he paused, memories dancing across his mind. "I did enjoy the work, and I genuinely loved my colleagues, but no. I don't regret leaving, just how I left. It ended badly, and it didn't have to. And that was in no small part my fault."

He took a cleansing breath and shook his head clear of the memories.

"And I dearly love serving this community," he finished. "I've never felt at home anywhere else. But here… this town feels like home. If I can bring a bit of light into the lives of these good folk through some kind words, guidance, and a helping hand, so much the better. 'The darker the night, the brighter the stars. The deeper the grief, the closer is God,'" he quoted.

Noting her expression, he shrugged, a little embarrassed.

"Dostoevsky," he explained.

"You're an interesting man, Reverend Jarrett,"

she said.

He realized she was still watching him intently. Rather than make him uncomfortable, he found his own gaze drawn toward hers like a round stone to the bottom of a hill.

Standing quickly, she broke the connection, and he felt something inside snap back almost painfully. Turning the handle, she drew the bucket up from the well.

Rue dipped a hand into the bucket, cupping it and raising a little water to her lips. She repeated the gesture a few times, then tipped the bucket just a touch in his direction, offering him some.

He smiled, removed his gloves, and hooked the bucket with two fingers, tipping it slightly further so he could reach in. After a few drinks from his palm, he let go with the two fingers he'd used to tip the bucket toward him.

She was still holding the other side, and his unexpected release of it caused it to bounce back toward her just slightly, but enough to cause a small splash of water to leap from it and into her eye.

Rue gasped in shock and outrage, blinking furiously, and Thomas froze.

"I'm so sorr—" he started, but she reached into the bucket and splashed a handful of water his way.

He blinked in surprise, looking down at the moisture on his black shirt. He looked back up at her.

In her eyes wasn't anger, it wasn't irritation, it

wasn't even smugness. It was a hesitant playfulness, and a measured calculation. A strange combination, but he understood it. She was testing him.

Well, she clearly wanted to see how he'd respond to a challenge. If she wanted it, she'd get it.

Thomas scooped a handful of water out and flung it at her. As she looked up at him, expression full of righteous indignation, her eyes danced.

He gave her a superior, daring look.

She looked at the bucket. He looked at the bucket. Their eyes met.

They both lunged for the bucket at the same instant, each trying to wrest control of it from the other.

In seconds, both were laughing as they fiercely struggled against one another. The water in the bucket was sloshing about wildly, splashing out in all directions, most of it ending up on Thomas and Rue.

"Rue!" a horrified voice called.

They both froze like a pair of misbehaving children caught by their mother. They looked at each other, then over to Josie.

Her expression was scandalized, but he couldn't help noticing a sparkle in the woman's eyes.

Thomas abruptly let go and stepped back, pointlessly brushing off his soaked clothes with his hands.

"I apologize, Mrs. Briggs. Your sister was helping me get a drink, and we had a bit of a mishap," he explained lamely. Surely, she'd seen the whole thing. He looked to Rue. "Thank you for your help, Miss Briggs. If you'll excuse me, I believe I have an appointment with Mrs. Taylor and Mrs. Rigby."

Rue's serious, chastened expression slipped and a giggle escape. It was possibly the most endearing sound he'd ever heard. She quickly put the serious face back on, though.

"Good day, ma'am," he said, tipping his hat to her, then again to her sister. "Mrs. Briggs."

Walking quickly, he circled back around the front of the house where his horse waited.

He wasn't at all sure what had just happened. It had escalated so quickly. Not the roughhousing, that tended to escalate. The connection. They'd gone from coolly civil to laughing and playing like a couple of children in the span of less than half an hour.

Whatever had happened, he thought, he couldn't let it happen again.

It couldn't happen again.

Chapter Eight

"It's just peculiar," Marshall said, eyes trained on the sky over the trees. Rue stood beside him and Robbie, shading her eyes from the sun as she looked where he was pointing.

In the distance, a flock of birds circled.

"Why is that odd?" she asked him.

"They're scavengers. They don't do that unless there's carrion."

"How do you know that?" she asked curiously.

"I read it in one of the books we brought," he said proudly.

"So, there's carrion over there?" she asked. "Why is that peculiar?"

"Because I don't think that's in the woods. Or even in Mr. Dalton's fields. I think that's right over his house," Marshall said pointedly.

Rue frowned, squinting at the birds again.

"Maybe he's butchering one of his animals?" she suggested. He shook his head.

"No, look," he said, pointing. She looked. "Some of the birds are going down, and then others are coming up. If Mr. Dalton was there, they wouldn't be going down there yet, they'd stay away, right?"

He had a point. It was peculiar.

"Do you suppose everything's all right?" Robbie asked softly from her other side.

The moment he asked the question, she got a feeling in her gut that it wasn't.

"I'm sure it is," she lied, "but let's go check on Mr. Dalton anyway. Just to make sure."

"Yeah," Robbie agreed.

"Robbie, go get the rifle," she told him, still watching the birds. Both boys looked at her in surprise.

"Do you think we'll need it?" Marshall asked.

"No, but I'd rather have it and not need it than the other way 'round. Marshall, go saddle the horses."

It suddenly seemed very important that they go check on Mr. Dalton.

Josie, Georgia, and the littler kids were all down by the stream, so when Robbie returned with the rifle, which he gave to her, she sent him down to let his mother know where they were heading.

He got back about the same time Marshall came around with the horses. They only had the two, so Robbie and Marshall would ride together.

The three of them set off at a trot. It wasn't far, thankfully, as the sun was already dipping in the sky. If something had happened, they didn't want to be out here after dark. Not with the Indians around.

They approached the farmhouse from the side, coming out from between the trees on a light trail that ran between their houses. The birds were definitely interested in something on the far side of the house, but from here, they couldn't tell what.

A sense of foreboding filled her. She shouldn't have brought the boys, she thought. This could be dangerous. Too late now, though. They were safer with her than alone.

She'd given the gun to Marshall. She'd never fired a rifle in her life, and Marshall was a responsible and reliable boy. He was also familiar with the gun and had been target shooting with it a few times since they moved here. He wasn't an ace shot, but at least he could hit a target more often than not.

Robbie, riding behind Marshall, held his brother about the waist. Marshall's expression was as cautious as hers, and he held the rifle ready. Not up, but definitely ready.

He guided the horse expertly with his knees. She wished she knew how he did that.

Rounding the back of the house, they saw what had the birds so excited. Robbie gasped, Marshall's rifle came up quickly, and Rue suppressed a scream.

Mr. Dalton lay belly down across a fence rail. Even from here, she could tell he was dead. Blood stained the grass beneath him, and the top of his head was a bloody mess.

"Stay here," she told the boys.

Marshall scanned the surrounding fields, gun aimed out into the distance.

Rue dismounted and ran to Mr. Dalton, wanting to check to see if he was alive, though she instinctively knew he wasn't.

From the look of him, he'd been shot in the back trying to run back to the house. Blood soaked the back of his shirt, though far more was on the ground beneath him, and she could see at least five bullet holes. But it was his head that horrified her most.

He'd been scalped.

"Robbie, get on my horse! Marshall, ride hard and get the sheriff! Give me the gun." She ran over to him and took the rifle, helping Robbie down from behind his brother.

Marshall immediately kicked the bay mare into a hard run, racing like his life depended on it. His might not, she thought, but the rest of theirs might.

Not wanting to disturb the scene, she returned to Robbie on her horse. He looked scared. She mounted behind him, holding him as much for comfort as for support.

She kept her eyes scanning their surroundings, ready to ride and ride hard if she saw or heard any sign of Indians.

Reverend Jarrett was wrong, she thought. The Tsawi weren't harmless at all. First, Dennis O'Leary had been attacked, and now this. A shudder of terror surged through her. They were right between the two attack sites, right on the edge of the tall plains the Indians called home.

She felt an irrational desire for the reverend to be there right at that moment. Why, she couldn't have said, but she knew without doubt that if he were here, she wouldn't be afraid.

Which was silly, because he was a priest. He wasn't allowed to fight. But she knew if he were here, he'd take care of everything.

"Don't worry, Aunt Rue," Robbie said comfortingly, rubbing the arm she had around him.

He didn't explain why she shouldn't worry, but the words and his touch helped anyway. She gave him a squeeze, keeping her eyes on the horizon.

It seemed to take forever for Sheriff Rawlins to arrive, but when he did, he came at full speed. He rode in from the long, dirt road to the side, his deputy by his side, Marshall right behind them.

Both men had their hands on their guns, looking around carefully as they rode.

Reaching her, the pair looked over at the body. Marshall came around to her other side, both he and his horse breathing hard.

"Aw, Dennis," muttered the deputy sadly. They had been friends, she realized from his tone.

"Miss Briggs. Coroner is on his way," the sheriff said. "Thanks for letting us know about this. You and the boys should head on home. We've got things under control from here."

"Under control?" Rue asked, feeling the hysteria build.

Rough customers, she could handle. The idea of being scalped by Indians terrified her beyond anything she'd ever known.

"The O'Leary place was attacked yesterday, and now Mr. Dalton is dead!" she continued. "We're right smack in the middle of this, sheriff. We can't stay on our land with this going on!"

"Now don't go running off half-cocked," the sheriff admonished. "There's certainly trouble right now, but we're not even sure what it is. This isn't the Tsawi's work."

"I don't care whose work it is, my family is in danger! What are we supposed to do while you figure things out?"

"Ma'am, I'm riding out right after this to speak to the Tsawi. We'll figure this out right away. Meantime, do you have any relatives nearby you can stay with?"

"We don't have any relatives anywhere, anymore," she said darkly.

"I'm mighty sorry to hear that," he replied. "Then my next suggestion would be to go to the church. Wouldn't be the first time the good reverend has put someone up for a day or two in tough times."

Her heart abruptly tried to go in three different directions at once; into her throat, down to the pit of her stomach, and right out of her chest.

"We couldn't possibly," she began.

"You can and should," Sheriff Rawlins argued. "You aren't wrong that you can't stay at your place. Not until we figure this out. Go back home, gather the rest of your family and some supplies, and head to the church."

"If we don't?" she asked, more out of fear than a challenge.

Though fear of what, she wasn't sure. All she knew was that she wasn't sure if she preferred facing the Indians or the church.

And the reverend.

"Well, ma'am, that's certainly up to you folks. I sure wouldn't risk it with my family, but that's me. You do as you like, but I will ask you again to head on back to your farm. This here is no place for a woman and two children."

"Children?" Marshall started indignantly, about to get a good set-to row going, but Rue threw him a glare that shut him up.

"We're leaving. Please let us know when we're safe to return home. We'll be at the church."

Josie would lose her mind, she knew. She was so determined to get this old farm up and running again. Having to leave it again for an indefinite amount of time was something that would cut her deeply.

She wanted so badly to build a life for the kids here. She wanted them to have stability and comfort, like they hadn't had since their father had died.

There was no help for it, though, Rue knew. They had to keep the children safe.

She gave the rifle back to Marshall, and the trio headed back home. Marshall kept a sharp eye out, but Rue found her thoughts wandering.

Reverend Jarrett would take them in. She had no doubt of that. But whether he would do so for true generosity's sake or to maintain his cover as a preacher, she didn't know.

At the very least, she'd have the opportunity to learn more about him, and maybe figure out the puzzle he presented. Provided she could keep her focus.

Which she would, she told herself.

Really.

Her stomach flipped a little at the idea of spending so much time at the church, but her heart flipped a little at the idea of spending so much time around Reverend Jarrett. Viciously, she pushed down both feelings.

Both were irrational.

And the latter was possibly dangerous. Especially if the reverend turned out to be a wolf in sheep's clothing. She'd seen the darkness slip back into his eyes just before he'd left their farm the day before. The way he'd laughed and played with her, though…

She hadn't played like that, or any way at all, really, in years. It wasn't her style. But something about him seemed to reach beyond the walls she'd built, beyond the years of hard living, and touch something purer, more innocent, deep within.

And when he'd laughed, his eyes had lit up like the full moon in a clear sky.

But even then, those eyes held a hardness, a sharpness, she couldn't identify.

A hawk, she corrected suddenly. With those eyes, a hawk was a better mental image for him than a wolf. He wasn't a wolf in sheep's clothing, he was a hawk among the pigeons.

His eyes were absolutely striking. Their steely gray color was unusual, sure, but it was the depth and power in them that seemed to call to her.

She felt as if…

Stop that at once, she chided herself. She needed to focus on protecting and caring for her family. That's all this was about, and all it would remain about.

Rue sighed. It was going to be a long couple of days.

For more than one reason.

Chapter Nine

Sitting astride Lady, his smoky gray mare, Thomas rode quickly. He had some distance to travel, so he wasn't riding her as hard as he knew she was capable, but he wasn't wasting any time, either.

He'd spoken with the sheriff already. On the merit of his friendship with the Tsawi, he'd convinced the sheriff to let him go speak to them first.

Thomas knew about Mr. Dalton and the circumstances surrounding his death. Dalton hadn't been killed by the Tsawi. He knew this without any doubt. But that was the rumor in town, and he could sense the tension and anger building. A veritable war would break out soon if nothing changed. A war the townsfolk would lose. Badly. The Tsawi weren't hostile, but they were excellent fighters when pushed to it. They didn't seek violence, but wouldn't shy away from it, either.

Lady nickered softly. She was a good horse. He'd had her for more than ten years, and she'd never failed him. He'd grown quite attached to her, too. Honestly, he doubted she'd behave half as well for anyone else. She was a highly spirited animal. But they understood each other.

The grasslands flowed by smoothly, a seemingly unbroken blanket of tall grass, waving gently in the wind. The effect resembled a green ocean, waves gently rolling across its surface.

But, like an ocean, he knew predators lurked somewhere out of sight. He could almost taste it. It was a slightly acrid tang to the air, nearly electric. Tension was high out here, and that always spoke of trouble.

Thomas was unarmed. He always was these days. God Himself couldn't make him hold a pistol in his hands again.

He'd ridden for hours when he sensed them. By old reflex, his hand slapped his hip, but touched only the leather of his belt instead of the metal his reflexes expected. Instead, he took a deep breath and whispered a prayer for protection and peace.

He slowed Lady, then stopped her. Dismounting, he held both arms out wide to his side, palms open and forward. Ten paces out from his horse, he stopped.

The only sound was the gentle rush of the wind through the tall grass. It stood taller than his navel. He knew from experience that a hundred Tsawi braves could be hiding in that grass within a few dozen yards of him, and he'd never see them. The absolute silence confirmed his suspicions even before the braves rose silently all around him.

The razor-tipped flint arrowheads all aimed his way called to mind the image of a thorn bush. But like a thorn bush, he thought, they would only pierce if you messed with them.

Which he had no intention of doing.

He spoke firmly, but gently, in their own native tongue of Caddo, taught to him by Storm-Chaser many years ago.

"Calm, friends. I seek peace and brotherhood by the fire of your chief."

One of the braves to his right replied angrily.

"Your people kill our people, and now you seek peace?"

Thomas paused, taken aback. The Tsawi had been attacked, too? And they thought the townsfolk were responsible?

"My people were attacked, as well. A good man has died. The people of my village believe it was the Tsawi. I know better. Your chief is my friend. Please, let me speak with him."

"How do we trust your words, white man?" the brave almost snarled.

"I speak for him," came a second voice.

Thomas looked over his shoulder to see a brave pushing through the crowd, his hands gently lowering bows around him as he passed.

"Red Feather? You speak for this white man?" asked the young brave.

Red Feather just stepped up to Thomas and

embraced him. Thomas returned the hug and smiled.

"It's good to see you, Red Feather."

"And you, Jarrett."

Bows lowered all around at this warm greeting by their respected brother. The first brave to speak didn't look happy.

"I need to speak to Owl," Thomas said. Red Feather nodded.

"Yes, you do. Come, my friend," Red Feather said, gesturing him forward. The crowd of braves parted, and Thomas followed.

He gave a short, sharp whistle, and Lady came trotting up behind him, following obediently. Red Feather chuckled.

"You have not gotten this horse shot yet? She is too good for you," Red Feather joked.

"She sure is," Thomas laughed, "but I try to take good care of her. We haven't been shot at in three years."

"Three years? I don't believe that. How do they not want to shoot you in that white village? You've been there for a long time."

Thomas laughed again. "They're good folk, Red Feather. They're not keen on shooting anybody."

Red Feather's expression darkened.

"Then it is not your people who have killed Stone Bow and Coyote?"

"Coyote was killed?" Thomas asked in pained

surprise. Coyote had been another friend of his.

"Yes. He died trying to save Stone Bow, who had already been shot."

"Noble," Thomas said. Red Feather nodded his agreement. "Were they able to kill any of their attackers?"

"No. They were shot from a very long way off. They perhaps did not even see their killers."

"How do you know it was someone from the village, then?"

"We've seen traces of a white man's raiding party the last few days. Our people are not so sloppy."

"But from the village?" Thomas pressed.

"No. But our people are afraid. Like your people think the Tsawi killed your man, even though they see none of my people. Our people see signs of white men killing our people, and they think our neighbors are responsible."

"There's precedent for that," Thomas agreed grudgingly. The white man had not been kind to the true people of the Americas.

"Yes, but I know it is not your people."

"How do you know that?"

"I have seen that village of yours. No one there could make the shots that killed Stone Bow and Coyote. Not even you."

Thomas frowned, considering this. He was a good shot with a rifle, though nothing like his friend Santiago. Nobody was anything like Santiago. But

Red Feather was right. Nobody in Granada had any skill as a sniper. And nobody in Granada would benefit from starting a war with the Tsawi, either.

If the Tsawi mobilized in anger, they'd wipe out half the town before any alarm could be raised at all. Someone in Granada starting a fight with the Tsawi would effectively be committing suicide. And so, he thought, it couldn't be someone from Granada.

They made it over a low rise, and the Tsawi village spread out below them. Thomas smiled. He'd never actually been to their village, though he and Owl went all the way back to his Saints days.

The normal bustle and noise of the small, active village faded quickly when he was spotted. Red Feather was right. The Tsawi were frightened. Especially of the white man right now.

Red Feather put an arm around Thomas's shoulders in a companionable fashion, and the people below relaxed somewhat. They still eyed him as he passed, though, mothers stepping in front of their children protectively.

Sitting by a cold firepit near the middle of the village sat Singing Owl, tying an arrowhead to a shaft. He saw Thomas, and his wrinkled, weather face split into a grin. He was missing several teeth, making his grin almost comical. Thomas returned the grin and stepped toward his friend.

Owl stood and embraced Thomas.

"Ah, my friend. It has been a long time," Owl said.

"It's good to see you, Owl. It has been too long."

"I would ask why you come, but I think I know. You come because of Coyote."

"I just learned about Coyote, Owl. I'm saddened to hear about it. He was a good man," Thomas said softly. Owl snorted.

"He was a mischief-maker and lots of trouble to his chief." Owl paused and grew more somber. "I shall miss him terribly. And Stone Bow was one of our best warriors. We shall all miss him, as well."

Thomas nodded. "I've come because our people are being killed, as well. And some effort is being made to make it look like your people are responsible."

Owl hesitated, then gestured for Thomas to sit. He did so.

"Do you think Coyote and Stone Bow were killed in revenge?"

"No, I don't." Thomas said firmly. Owl frowned and looked at him in surprise. "Nobody in my village has any animosity toward your people, Owl. Nobody there could make the shots Red Feather told me about. And nobody there would be so foolish as to start a war with your tribe. They wouldn't stand a chance, and the sheriff and mayor both know it."

"You speak wisely. What, then, do you think?" Owl asked after a moment's consideration.

"I think someone outside is trying to start a war

between your people and mine. Maybe just my town, but maybe more. I don't know yet. But they want your people to think we're at fault, and my people to think yours are. Neither is true."

"I agree. This makes sense. But why us? Why here? It would not be much of a fight."

"No, it wouldn't. And you wouldn't stay in the town once you'd finished, so the only possible gain from this is either to start enough trouble that the government sends the army in to wipe you out, or that the village itself is wiped out. Or both. I just can't figure out why. Neither of us sit on land rich in resources. And certainly not of any strategic value. Who gains from this?"

"Not my people," Owl said firmly.

"Nor mine," Thomas agreed. They were both quiet a minute before Thomas spoke again. "I want you to promise me something, Owl."

"Of course, my friend," Owl replied.

"Tell your people they're not to harm mine."

"I cannot make that promise, Jarrett, and you know it," Owl admonished. Thomas sighed.

"I know. At least tell them not to harm any of my people unless my people shoot first. And then only the ones doing the shooting."

"This I can agree to," Owl said with a nod. "But you must make the same promise to me."

"Already done, but I'll say it again. And again, as often as I must."

"We do not want a war with your people,

Jarrett."

"I know, Owl. I know. Your people and the people of Granada have lived peacefully alongside each other for years. We've both benefitted. Can you have your scouting parties look for signs of an encampment nearby?" he added as a thought came to him. "If there's a group around here hassling us both, they can't be more than half a day's ride out, since they've been back every day for several days."

"We will do that. They were looking for your people coming out toward us already, but I will have them look for white men camped outside your village."

"If they find anything, don't move on them without both your full force and the element of surprise. The men we're dealing with are extremely dangerous. A scouting party, maybe even two or three, wouldn't stand a chance. Thank you, Owl."

"I understand, and you are welcome. Will you stay with us tonight?" Owl asked. Thomas smiled.

"No, thank you. My people are frightened and need their minister there for comfort," Thomas replied. Owl shook his head with a wry smile.

"They say a black raven is always black, Jarrett, but you have changed much since we first met. You're the brightest black raven I know. How you became a white man's preacher, I'll never know."

"The Lord works in mysterious ways," Thomas grinned. Owl laughed.

"Fine, then. Take your clichés and be away with

you. I have to finish making arrows to replace the new ones stolen from Stone Bow's body."

"The killers took Stone Bow's arrows?" Thomas asked. Owl nodded. "That explains where the arrows came from. The first sighting of tracks had half a broken arrow near them. Mr. Dalton's farm had a few lying around, as well. None of them looked like they'd been fired."

"The ones responsible for this are trying hard to fool your people," Owl noted. Thomas nodded.

"It might have worked, too, except the sheriff and I know the Tsawi too well for that."

Owl nodded. "Yes, their law man is a good man. You will tell him we spoke?"

"I will," Thomas agreed.

"Good. With Red Feather leading the scouts and you two leading the white men of your village, we will find these serpents."

"How quickly can your warriors be ready to ride?" Thomas asked.

Without responding, Owl turned his head and whistled, loud and sharp. There was a flurry of motion in the village, and in seconds, Thomas had thirty armed men around them, bows all pointed at him.

Thomas stared at his friend in surprise. Owl began laughing hysterically. It was several moments before Owl calmed enough to wave down his men, who turned and vanished again between the packed-earth lodges.

"All right, you old weasel," Thomas said with a laugh. "Just be sure to have them ready if we find the raiders and they're more than the sheriff can handle."

"Don't worry, white man. If we find them first, there will be nothing left for your sheriff to handle."

"I believe you," Thomas said, standing. Singing Owl stood, as well.

The old man embraced his friend, who returned it warmly.

"Come back to visit, Jarrett. When all this is finished," Owl added. "We will celebrate the change of the seasons when the moon is new. You may join us. Some of the braves do not yet know your legend."

"By the grace of God, old friend, they never will," Thomas said somberly as he turned to walk away. "I'll be back with the new moon. Fair warning!" he called back over his shoulder.

Singing Owl laughed behind him.

Chapter Ten

Reverend Jarrett had been gone from the church when they'd arrived. Nobody seemed quite sure where he'd gone, so Rue and the family had spent some time in town while they waited.

It took a few hours, but he came riding into town on the main road toward the church. They spotted him immediately.

Rue's heart skipped at least a few beats when her eyes found him. He rode comfortably, almost absently, but with an easy grace that to her experienced eye spoke of years in the saddle.

"Reverend!" Josie called. She held up a hand to invite him over when he looked up. He smiled and steered his beautiful, gray horse their way.

"Afternoon, ladies, gentlemen," he said, tipping his hat to each in turn.

"Good afternoon, reverend," Josie said. "I hate to trouble you, but we have a mighty big favor to ask of you."

The reverend dismounted and stepped over. She noticed he didn't tie the reins off to anything, just draped them casually across the saddle. She also noticed that the horse didn't move from the spot he'd left it.

"Of course!" he said with a nod. His smile had faded at the seriousness of her tone, but his focus and sincerity hadn't.

God, those eyes, she thought. They pierced like bullets, but with a light to them she couldn't justify against their steeliness.

Those eyes turned to her, and she felt suddenly laid bare. Except he clearly couldn't see everything she hid within, because she could see the puzzlement in them, too. Much like her own when she gazed at him, she imagined.

She could also see the hesitation. He wasn't sure where they stood after their scuffle at the well. Neither was she, if it came to that.

Not that it mattered, she reminded herself firmly. He was a priest. That was where he stood. And she stood in his congregation, and even that not by choice. No more, no less.

"Well, what with the attack at the O'Leary's, and then with Mr. Dalton's…" Josie choked back the word.

Rue heard Robbie whimper slightly and reached out to hold his hand. He didn't resist, a sure sign he was upset.

Reverend Jarrett nodded, indicating she didn't need to say it.

"Well, we don't feel quite safe 'round our land

right now. Sheriff Rawlins suggested we might, that is, maybe we could…"

"You need shelter," he said simply.

Josie nodded, clearly embarrassed, and the reverend smiled. The smile reached his eyes, Rue saw with an unexpected swell of relief. She'd been watching for that without realizing it. The sharpness was still there. It was always there. But the smile wasn't fake. It reached his eyes. That was significant.

That smile turned her way and her traitorous heart fluttered again. The angle of his jaw, the faint trace of dark stubble, the strong nose and expressive mouth… He was striking in every regard, not just his eyes, she thought.

Rue immediately chastised herself. This wasn't the time, the place, nor the man over whom to get all girly, she grumbled inwardly. Hundreds of men come and gone in her life, and it was a blasted preacher that got her heart skipping. Didn't that just beat all…

"The Lord's house is open to all," he said with a gesture toward the church. "Night or day," he added with a wink. "I was going to fix up some stew for dinner. Nothing fancy, but it's easy enough to feed a crowd with that."

"Oh, you don't have to do that," Josie protested.

"It's my pleasure, truly. We were going to have dinner together this week anyway, remember? We'll just do it a few days early. I'll make my famous biscuits tomorrow, and we can cook up some chicken. It's easy enough to go shopping if it looks as though you'll be staying a mite longer than that."

"That really does sound wonderful," Josie agreed. "Thank you so much."

"No trouble," he replied.

"Don't be so modest, we're a lot of trouble," Rue interjected, speaking for the first time.

His eyes turned to her, and she saw something in them unexpected. A surge of warmth. And not just the one in her own stomach.

"No trouble that I mind," he conceded with a twinkle in his eye. "If you're ready, I'm headed back to the church now."

"We're ready," Marshall said. "Come on folks, let's load up."

The ladies let the boy take charge, trading an affectionate look with one another over his efforts. They all piled into the wagon, and Marshall clicked his tongue, the wagon moving out into the street.

Reverend Jarrett mounted and steered his horse easily over to walk slowly alongside the wagon.

"Why were you gone?" Lucy asked with childish frankness.

"Lucy, it's not polite to ask someone such questions. The reverend's business isn't ours," Rue chastised.

"I don't mind, Miss Briggs, truly." The reverend's rich baritone did nothing to help cool the heat building in her chest. "Miss Lucy, I was out speaking to the Tsawi chief."

Both boys whipped their heads around to stare at him in awe.

"Truly?" asked Marshall.

"Yes, sir," the reverend replied. "Good man."

"And what did you discover, if I may ask?" Josie inquired.

"Mostly just confirmation of what I already knew. It isn't the Tsawi, or any of the Pawnee tribes responsible for the attacks. They're being framed. I knew that already. Two of their people have been killed, too, in a way that implicates the townsfolk. I hadn't known that."

"But the people here would never…" Rue argued, trailing off, realizing she didn't actually know the people here that well. For all she knew, the whole town could be populated by cannibals.

"No, they wouldn't," Reverend Jarrett agreed. "They think it's white folk, but not from our town. They've got scouting parties out now, looking for an encampment. Seems to me someone is trying to turn us against the Tsawi, and vice versa. I just can't figure why. In any case, you're in no danger from the Tsawi unless you start shooting at them first. I have the chief's word."

"So, we can go home?" Robbie asked eagerly.

"I wouldn't suggest that," Reverend Jarrett replied. She might have been mistaken, but Rue was sure she saw his eyes flicker to her for an instant. "The Tsawi might not be responsible for the attacks, but someone is. And it's someone who's looking for trouble and doesn't mind taking a life for their own ends. Your land is plum in the middle of the recent attacks. Best you stick with me until we can sort this all out. Don't worry, Robbie. God and I will take care of you."

"It really is awfully kind of you," Josie said. He laughed.

"We'll both get tired quickly, if you keep thanking me. It's part of my job to look out for the parish, including providing shelter and supplies when necessary. I'm here to support the community. Spiritually, emotionally, physically…"

"Well, it is appreciated," Josie said.

"There you go again. Does she always thank people this much?" he asked, turning to Rue.

Rue laughed. "Yes," she said simply. "You should have heard her going on when I arrived from Kansas City."

"Oh, stop," Josie protested laughingly. "I can't help it if you folks keep doing such kind and generous things for me. I'm starting to feel quite helpless, really."

"Nonsense, Mrs. Briggs," Jarrett argued. "When you lost your husband, God rest his soul, you rounded up six children and brought them to a new town where you knew no one and are rebuilding a fallow farm all on your own. Nobody can call you helpless."

"Not alone," Josie said, glancing at Rue. Jarrett

immediately tipped his hat her way.

"No offense meant, Miss Briggs. Your help is no small thing indeed. I meant only that she is doing this without a father for her children. I can't imagine there's any other role you couldn't fill as needed for the family."

"None taken, reverend," Rue answered. She appreciated that he wasn't discounting her value here, or even implying that they needed a man around to get anything done. "It isn't an easy adventure, but we're making the best of it."

"That you are, Miss Briggs. I greatly admire the whole family's determination and strength. This latest episode is just another hitch on the road to building your lives here. Few things are ever easy, but I assure you, raising a family here is worth it."

"I'm relieved to hear it, Reverend Jarrett," Josie said honestly.

"Marshall, take the wagon around the side yard, if you wouldn't mind," he directed. Marshall nodded and steered around the side of the church.

There was a small garden around the side, and a small, fenced pasture behind it. He dismounted and began caring for his horse, offering direction for where Marshall should put their things.

It wasn't long until they were all walking through the small side door and into what appeared to be his private rooms. She could see a small door to one side, leading to a small bedroom. The rest was one larger room, with a small table and a few chairs, some cupboards, a wash basin, and a stove. To one side, a comfortable-looking padded armchair sat. It was near a small window, and the side table beside it held an oil lantern and, unexpectedly, a book.

Rue was interested to note the book wasn't the Bible. It was, to her surprise, *Anna Karenina*. The strip of soft leather being used as a bookmark was just over two-thirds of the way through the novel. He hadn't been lying. He really was a reader.

She was also unsurprised to find the place was immaculate. It was swept, dusted, and with everything in its place. It was sparse, but comfortable.

"I thought we could put the ladies and young Thomas in the bed, the two young men out here in bedrolls, with the girls in bedrolls back in the bedroom with you ladies. Although I'm certainly open to suggestions, if you've got a better arrangement in mind?" Jarrett finished, raising a brow in question.

Rue considered for a moment.

"Where will you sleep?" she asked, and immediately regretted the question when the barest hint of mischief sparked in his eyes.

Whatever taunt he was about to make, he obviously suppressed, though, because he replied "Don't you worry about me. I've got an old hammock I plan to hang out between the cottonwoods outside the door."

Rue admired his restraint, but she couldn't deny she was dying to hear what playful remark had flickered behind his eyes at her question. This man apparently hid a playful side right along with that mysterious darkness.

"You can't be serious," Josie protested. "We can't put you out of your own home!"

"Don't fret, Mrs. Briggs. It's my pleasure to help, and my pleasure to sleep under the stars. It's been a long time since I've had a night like that, and I find myself looking forward to the excuse. For now, though, let's get some chow on for the little ones."

He began moving about in the small kitchen with a confidence and ease that impressed her. Rue sat in the padded armchair while the boys carried in the few belongings they'd packed. Rue watched him as he worked.

Jarrett hummed idly, a tune she didn't recognize. His movements in the kitchen were smooth and sure, and everything he did had a peculiar grace to it. It was almost feline.

In no time, he had washed his hands, had a fire going in the stove, and a rolling boil in the pot on the stovetop. His obvious comfort in the kitchen was oddly appealing. Jarrett had unexpected skills, she thought.

Reverend Jarrett, she corrected herself in annoyance. When had she started thinking of him as Jarrett? It was a dangerous thing to lose his title. She might forget who, and what, he actually was.

He turned, and she caught glimpse of the white tab on his collar. Never mind, she thought. Precious little chance of forgetting who he is.

Jarrett pulled a few things out of a cupboard and began adding things to the stew. He diced meat and vegetables smoothly and quickly and was unhesitating in adding seasonings into the pot. The aromas of the spices reached her nose and her mouth instantly began to water.

"There we are," he said, dusting his hands against one another. "Give that a little time, and we'll be in business. I thought we could eat it as a picnic under the cottonwoods, if that sounds all right. There's not much space at the table here, I'm afraid."

"That sounds lovely, Reverend Jarrett," Josie said.

"Do you have enough bowls and spoons?" Rue asked. He smiled at her. She pounded the swelling feeling in her heart down.

"Spoons, I have more than enough. The confounded things seem to multiply in the drawer all on their own. I truly have no idea where most of them came from." He chuckled, and Rue couldn't help but grin. "As for bowls, I don't have enough of those, but I figure the little ones could use mugs. The handle will make it easier for them while trying to eat outside, anyway."

"That's a really good idea," she admitted.

It was impossible not to like that man, she thought in irritation. He was kind and generous, and sweet-natured, as well as thoughtful, easygoing, and disarmingly charming. His chiseled features certainly didn't hurt, either, she thought ruefully. If he weren't a priest, maybe… No!

That is quite enough of that line of thought, she berated herself for perhaps the thousandth time. Even if he weren't a priest, he wouldn't want her. Not with her past.

"I'm afraid I don't have anything to go along with the stew. I wasn't expecting company."

"Oh, don't even fret about it, Reverend Jarrett," Josie said. "We're just so pleased to be here."

"Well, it's a pleasure having you here, but I'm sure you'd be more comfortable at home. It's a bit tight here for eight of you. With a little luck, we'll have the issues out by your place sorted in no time, and you all can get back to settling in."

Rue hoped for the same, but for at least one reason that was all her own.

Chapter Eleven

The sun was warm for the time of year, the sky clear and the kind of blue that begs to be gazed at. Rue walked along the old deer trail between the trees, watching the patches of blue between the overhead branches.

Jarrett had been gone when she and the family had awakened that morning, despite the whole lot of them being early risers. Well, except Rue, who was more of a night owl, although living with her sister and her kids was rapidly forcing a shift to her sleeping habits.

They had quickly vacated his apartments, Josie insisting they didn't want to loiter around the church and be under the good reverend's feet all day long. Rue thought that was an excellent idea, but for entirely different reasons.

Being around the man made her think unreasonable things. Heart-fluttering, foolish, impossible, unreasonable things. It was ridiculous, she knew, on at least three levels. She didn't need the hassle of trying to navigate a relationship right now, no man would want a woman like her with her past, and the confounded man in question was a priest from a celibate order.

She might as well be fawning over the King of Siam, for all the likelihood of anything happening here.

Except the King of Siam didn't make her heart skitter around in her chest like she was a moonstruck little schoolgirl.

She looked up as a jay called loudly from a nearby tree. The lightly wooded trail had a constant backdrop of gentle birdsong, but this jay in particular wanted to be sure any potential mates, apparently within a ten-mile radius, could hear him.

Keep it to yourself, she thought in what sounded even to her a petulant tone. Love was never worth it.

It had been a broken heart when she was seventeen that had led her to rush into an intimate encounter with the eldest son of the local butcher. When the affair had been discovered, the entire community had rallied against her, spreading first the truth, and then more and more egregious lies about her promiscuity. Her father had been outraged when he'd heard.

At her.

So much so that the man hadn't even wanted to hear her side of things, he'd simply believed every scandalous thing the public was saying. He'd very nearly thrown her from his house, though her sister

Josie had convinced him otherwise.

It wasn't long after that the butcher himself cornered her on an isolated street and demanded his own turn for a roll in the hay. She'd refused, of course, and when he'd tried to force her, she had clawed viciously at his face, drawing a surprising amount of blood.

Escaping from him, she'd run and hid, the large man screaming after her in rage and pain. She had remained hidden for nearly an hour before she was calm and brave enough to try and get home. But when she got within sight of her home, she saw the sheriff and a deputy at her doorstep, with the butcher himself, speaking angrily with her father.

Sneaking closer, she'd heard enough to realize that the butcher was accusing her of attempting to seduce him, and then attacking him when he'd virtuously refused. What was worse, both the sheriff and her father seemed not to question his story at all. Her reputation preceded her, apparently.

Knowing she had no prayer of defense, not when the entire town would believe every word of the butcher's story, she had run. With no money, no resources, no friends, no family, nowhere to go and nothing to do, she had run.

It had taken a bit of damsel-in-distress storytelling to con her way onto an outgoing caravan heading for Kansas City. It had been weeks on the street there before she'd been approached by a local madam with an offer of honest work. She'd found out later that the work intended involved a lot of lying down and pretending to have a good time.

Rue had run again, back to the streets, refusing to engage in such employ. Almost three more months passed before she went looking for the madam once more. Half-dead from starvation, having tried every legitimate means of earning money and lodging and failing in every instance due to her circumstance, there had been no doors left open to her. Save one.

She shook her head sadly. It hadn't been hard. Quite the contrary, to her surprise. All she had to do was not care, which three months of near starvation had facilitated quite handily.

But in so doing, every other door was permanently barred to her. No other jobs would take her, no man would take her for wife, and none would offer even charity to one of her station. She worked in the brothel, or she died. It was that simple.

And then, many years later, Josie's letter had arrived. Rue hadn't even known how Josie had found her, though she eventually learned that Josie had finally hired a Pinkerton detective to track her down.

In the letter, she had told Rue that her husband had passed, and that their father had died years before, leaving her alone with the children. Her husband had left a decent nest egg, having been a reasonably well-established merchant, but in the city, it wouldn't last more than a few years. Josie had shared her plan to have Rue come with her out to the country, where she had just bought a small farm.

The money left would hold them reasonably well for a year, maybe two, in the country, by which time they should be earning some income from the production of the farm.

The idea of rejoining her dear sister was too much to resist, despite the hardships and struggles she knew it would entail, and Rue had packed up her few belongings and meager savings and left in the early hours of the morning, telling no one.

She intended to spend the rest of her life with her sister, even after the children had grown and moved on. She had no one else, and nothing else. But it wasn't such a bad arrangement. She adored her sister, and the children, something she'd honestly been worried about. They could manage on the farm just fine indefinitely, she was sure, and she and Josie would take care of each other.

She rounded a bend in the deer trail as it curved toward what she now saw was a moderately-sized hot spring. Steam rose lazily from its surface, gentle ripples moving across its surface.

Rue smiled and walked toward the spring. Soaking her feet in the warm water sounded lovely, if the water wasn't too hot. She froze, still partially hidden from view by the trees.

The ripples in the water had changed, as if something stirred beneath the surface. She sidestepped behind a tree and watched in alarm. After a few moments, something broke the surface, rising up quickly.

As the steaming water fell from the figure, she recognized it. Or him, she corrected.

Jarrett now stood, naval-deep in the spring, running his hands across his face as he breathed deeply in and out; heavily enough that she knew he'd been under the water for some time.

His strong chest moved with his breath, water dripping down his surprisingly powerful figure, his well-toned arms reaching up as he slicked his hair back out of his eyes. His skin held a tinge of pink from the warmth of the water but was otherwise nicely tanned.

Rue's breath caught at the sight. If she'd had any doubts about the reverend's divinity, they vanished in that instant, though that divinity manifested in a very different way than she'd expected.

He reached down and splashed a little more water up across his face, shaking it off. He took a step in her direction and began to rise further out of the concealing water. She almost gasped.

Suddenly, he paused, not having emerged far enough to reveal anything more than she'd already seen and looked up into the trees toward her. She leaned further back behind the tree but was unable to look away completely.

"You can come out," he called. "I'm not armed

and have no money, though, so if you're looking for a fight or a lucrative robbery, I'm afraid you'll be disappointed."

Hesitating a moment, Rue stepped out from behind the trees and walked toward him. His surprise at seeing her was evident, but he didn't blush, try to hide, or move back into deeper water. She still couldn't see anything, for which she was sure they were both grateful at this moment, but she could see enough of his upper body to feel the flush in her own cheeks.

It baffled her, however. She'd seen hundreds of men's bodies over the years, some quite well formed, and none had flooded her with heat the way his did, despite the handful of scars visible from this vantage point. More pieces to the puzzle, she thought, trying to guess where they might have come from.

"Miss Briggs," he said calmly, though she could see his breathing was coming sharper than it had a moment ago. "How unexpected, though it is a marvelous day for a walk."

"It is indeed, Jarr… Reverend Jarrett."

Saying his title out loud and realizing how she was looking at him filled her with an unusual surge of embarrassment. It was so easy to forget his station when he looked like this.

"I'm impressed you found the old deer trail. It's not easy to spot, even from the tree line. Beautiful walk, though, and this spring is one of my favorite places to go for some quiet."

"I apologize, I'll leave you to your peace," she said, starting to turn away.

"No need," he answered. "I was just finished. I'll get out and dressed and the spring is all yours."

He waited a moment, obviously waiting see if she would turn away. When she didn't, the barest hint of a curve touched the corner of his lips, and a challenging look came into his eye as he stepped forward.

Involuntarily, Rue spun around an instant before he lifted out of the water, turning her back to him. Her eyes were wide, her breath rapid and shallow, and her heart was beating a staccato rhythm in her chest. God, she was acting like a naïve teenager, she thought with a wince.

She heard the splashing behind her as he came out of the spring, and despite her earlier involuntary turn, it took a great deal of effort not to turn back around again.

He rustled around behind her for a while before speaking.

"Miss Briggs, I'm quite decent again. The spring is all yours."

Rue turned, seeing him once more clothed in his usual black pants and shirt with the white collar. He was pulling on his dark boots, his hair still damp and slicked back on his head. God help her, he still looked striking.

His eyes, when he turned them back up to her,

held a distinct note of mischief that sent a tingle up her spine. It was a layer to him she hadn't expected existed.

"I don't mean to chase you off," she found herself saying. "I was only going to give my feet a little soak. If you… I mean, if you'd like to stay, I wouldn't mind the company."

She knew it was a dangerous thing to say. She was too drawn to this man as it was. Rue moved to sit on a solid ledge on one side of the pool, lifted the edge of her cream-colored skirt, and began unlacing her high, white boot.

Jarrett put down his foot, his own boot now secure, and regarded her a moment before nodding.

"That's mighty kind of you, Miss Briggs. I believe I shall." He stood and moved to a nearby stone, sitting within arm's reach of her.

She was quiet a long moment, unsure of what to say, but desperate to say something. Foolish though it was, she did not want him to leave. She asked the first thing that came to her mind.

"Are you still in touch with any of your former colleagues?" she asked.

Something about his seated position changed, tensed almost imperceptibly, and she immediately regretted the question. He was quiet a long moment before answering.

"A couple, though not actively. Jack rode through a few months back with his fiancée. Honored me by asking me to perform the ceremony. I've written letters to two of the others. As for the rest…" he hesitated, then seemed to give up and remained silent.

"What happened?" she asked.

She knew it wasn't her business, and that it was a sensitive subject, but her curiosity had grown to an unbearable level.

"One of my colleagues made a stupid decision. I got angry and overreacted. We all did. There was a fight, and someone got hurt. By me. It nearly broke me, and certainly broke us. I was lost a long time after that. Eventually, God helped me turn myself back around, though, and now I serve Him by serving His people."

"That's noble," she said softly.

There was so much more to this story than he was saying. She could hear it in his tone, if not his words.

Rue finished the removal of her second boot and eased her feet into the water. It was hot, but not unpleasantly so. It occurred to her that revealing her bare feet and legs to a man not her husband was generally not appropriate, though she'd shown a great deal more often enough that it didn't bother her.

Interestingly, he didn't seem overly concerned about it, either. One way or the other.

"More of a recompense than an act of nobility, really," he replied.

"I know that feeling," she said almost to

herself, thinking of her own work helping her sister and the children.

There was an element of recompense to her actions, too, trying to make up for abandoning her sister for so many years. She felt no guilt over her lifestyle, as she knew she wasn't given much of an option, but she held more than a small dose of guilt over having left her sister in that house without so much as a goodbye.

"I can't imagine you've done much needing recompense, Miss Briggs," he said.

"You'd be surprised, reverend," she retorted.

She knew without doubt he'd consider a great deal of repentance to be in order at the very least, if he had known anything of her past. Rue wasn't about to confess to him, though, priest or no priest.

He was quiet long enough that she looked at him. Those raptor eyes were focused so sharply on her she was surprised they didn't cut. The expression wasn't unkind, but she once again felt like he could see straight through to her core.

"No," he said finally. "I don't believe I would. You may have sinned, Miss Briggs, we all have, but I don't believe you've done harm."

"Maybe not on purpose," she hedged. Hurting her sister wasn't at all her intention with leaving, self-preservation was, but she still felt guilt over it.

"Ah, but that's quite a different can of beans, now, isn't it." It was a statement, not a question.

"Maybe," she said. She wasn't convinced, but it

warmed her that he'd say as much.

"May I ask you a personal question, Miss Briggs?"

"You can ask," she said, giving him a warning look.

"You don't care for the church much."

"That's not a question," she replied, looking away.

"No, but the why of it is," he said simply. "Your reaction to me was a little cool on both our first and second meeting, and you always seem a touch uncomfortable in the church, whether a sermon is going on or not. I'm just curious as to why exactly that is. I know I said it wasn't my business, so you can just tell me to drop it."

"I'd really rather not get into it," she said coolly. He nodded.

"Fair enough. I just hope you'll let me know if there's anything I can do to ease your discomfort. I'm only here to help, not to make anyone uneasy."

"Thank you, I will."

Reverend Jarrett was quiet again for a long moment, and when he spoke again, his voice was soft.

"For what it's worth, what you're doing for your sister and those children is quite noble. If you feel you need to offer recompense for past sins, I'd say you're doing a fine job of it. There's nothing more noble than helping others, especially when it's an inconvenience to yourself." He was quiet a moment, eyes locked on hers. When he spoke again, it was barely above a whisper. "You're a remarkable woman, Miss Briggs."

Rue looked at him again. His gaze was no less intense, but it was softer, and there was something in it that seemed to call to her. She was drawn toward those eyes, and they seemed to get bigger and deeper with each instant.

It was a full two seconds before she realized she'd actually leaned toward him, and another to realize he'd done the same. They were inches apart now, and she could feel his breath on her lips.

Her world faded away until only his eyes still existed.

As if the tension between them had been abruptly cut with a knife, he snapped back, eyes wide.

"Forgive me, Miss Briggs. I should go. Enjoy the spring. Good day." He stood, tipped his hat, and walked quickly back to the trail.

Rue released a breath she didn't realize she'd been holding and winced at a deep ache that suddenly appeared in her chest. She watched him go, and felt the ache sharpen.

What exactly just happened, she wondered.

Chapter Twelve

What exactly just happened, he wondered. They were fine, just talking, and only for a few minutes, and then suddenly... so suddenly...

God help me, he prayed. He had so far been able to deny his attraction, though not with much conviction. But after that moment by the spring, there was no more denial possible.

He walked quickly back to town, lost in a tailspin of self-doubt, frustration, and praying for guidance he didn't seem to be receiving.

Thomas didn't know what it was about her. He barely knew her at all. But there was something. It was more than physical. She was beautiful, yes, and he was attracted that way, but it was more than that.

The pull she had on him ached deep in his chest when he thought about her, which was more and more often by the minute, it seemed. There was a vibrance, a life in her eyes he had never seen before in any other woman.

He needed to explore this. No, he immediately corrected, he needed to pull as far back as humanly possible. He needed to maintain distance and propriety, boundaries and vows.

He needed to get her out of his home.

Determination replacing his frustration and confusion, Thomas hurried to the church and got his horse. Lady was eager for a run; he could tell by the way she reacted when she saw him.

Good, he thought. He needed a run, too.

Quickly saddling his mare, he mounted and trotted out of the stable yard. He'd push her into a run as soon as they were out of sight of the town proper. That would avoid unnecessary questions if someone saw him racing out of the churchyard as if the devil himself were on his tail.

Temptation certainly was, he thought.

Even at a run, reaching the Briggs's farm took a bit of time. He slowed before reaching the farm itself, letting Lady catch her breath. Here, he hoped he could find some clues to help him solve this puzzle and return the Briggs family to their own home.

Aside from the rustling of the gentle breeze across the fields and the chirping of the birds, all was quiet as he approached. It wasn't a comfortable silence. It was the kind that told his trained senses that all was not quite right.

For the millionth time, his fingers twitched, aching to hold the weight of cold iron in his hands again.

Habits long unused came to the fore once

more, and he found himself circling off the main road, taking to the brush on the side of the road. He dismounted by a patch of good, green grass, and encouraged Lady to graze here, out of sight of the road.

Staying low himself, he moved quietly and quickly through the fields toward the side of the Brigg's farm. Stalking wasn't his strongest suit, that was more Storm-Chaser's forte, but he was no slouch.

The nearer he got to the farmhouse, the more wrong everything felt. He paused and listened but heard nothing out of sorts. He scented the air, but smelled nothing unusual, either. Everything looked calm and quiet.

But Thomas, unlike many, didn't discount his instincts. He'd survived well over a hundred gunfights, ambushes, brawls, and a few all-out battles in his years, and had well earned his reputation as the deadliest gunfighter this side of the Mississippi. One didn't live long in his former professions, either as a killer for hire or a vigilante with the Saints of Laredo, without listening closely to instinct.

Something here was very wrong.

The house was quiet and dark, the mid-day sun casting few shadows and lending to the peculiarly unsettling air. He glanced in a few windows but saw no movement. All was still.

Moving out to the eastern side of the house, he

still saw nothing. But the nagging feeling remained. There was danger here, he was sure of it, he just couldn't see it.

Kneeling, he examined a patch of disturbed grass. It was a hoofprint. A fresh one. The horse was shod, and therefore not one of the Tsawi's, he knew. They didn't shoe their horses.

He moved in the direction the hoofprint indicated, looking closely at the ground as he went, while not looking away from his surroundings for more than a second at a time. There weren't many places on this side of the fields to hide for an ambush. The weed-covered field wasn't even waist high, there weren't many trees this side of the field, and the house itself he'd already circled. But lack of caution killed more people than the black plague.

Another hoofprint, right beside a human footprint. Crouching low, he examined the footprint. It was heavy, made by a big man, but clad in moccasin, not boot. But the step was clumsy, flat-footed, not like the careful heel-toe roll of a Tsawi scout or warrior. Between the shod horse and the flat-footed gait, the maker of this print was almost certainly a white man.

Why would a white man be wearing moccasins? A white man clearly not trained to move like the Tsawi. Or any tribe that he knew of. They all moved more carefully than this.

Thomas moved forward again, staying low. That tension in the air was setting his teeth on edge.

He'd have given anything to have Jack or Storm-Chaser here with him right now. Or any of the Saints, for that matter. Santiago, Lucky, or Kid Grady would all have made him feel better right at that moment.

Not that any of them would want to see him. He wasn't responsible for starting the fight that had broken the Saints, but he was unquestionably responsible for the end of it.

One day, when he'd worked up the courage, he would send a letter to others. Storm-Chaser had already forgiven him, as had Jack, though the two had never spoken of it again. But the others...

Santiago probably wouldn't. Lucky might. He was always quick to forgive a row, which was fortunate, as he got into so many. But Kid Grady? That bridge had burned beyond repair, Thomas knew.

Kid had started the fight, of that nobody doubted, but Thomas's reaction had divided the Saints down a hard line. Jack and Storm-Chaser had sided with him initially, Santiago and Lucky with Kid Grady. But it hadn't ended there, and in the end, Thomas had walked away. For good.

Jack and Storm-Chaser had left, too, he'd later learned. Jack had gone on to become a bounty hunter, though had recently settled down with Evie Delano, and Storm-Chaser had gone off on his own, as he was prone to doing anyway, likely to the Dakota territory up north.

Thomas spotted more tracks, from multiple horses and men. All the horses were shod, and all the men wore moccasins. None had the step of the Tsawi. He estimated perhaps a dozen men with as many horses, milling about in a small open patch of dirt.

Which also made no sense. If you were going to hide yourselves, as a scouting or hunting party might, why mill about in the only patch of ground nearby that would so neatly hold prints?

In the grass to one side, a splash of color caught his eye. He moved over, crouching down to pick up the shaft and tail of an arrow.

The fletching was definitely Tsawi.

Frowning, he wished he had the arrowhead the Briggs family had found. He had the oddest feeling that this shaft matched that arrowhead.

Re-examining the tracks, he confirmed again that these were fresh. So, someone had broken an arrow, dropped the head in one place, then returned days later to drop the tail end in a conspicuous place.

There was absolutely no doubt that these people were trying to frame the Tsawi and instill fear in the locals.

But why? To get them to turn on the Tsawi? The Army would intervene if it escalated to that level, and the Tsawi would be wiped out. The Tsawi were largely peaceful, though, and had been coexisting with the town for many years. Their land wasn't particularly rich in resources. At least, not any more so than any other land around here.

Or maybe to get the townsfolk to take a few shots at the Tsawi and get the Tsawi to wipe out the town. But again, why? The town wasn't particularly resource rich, either. The soil was good, but the best way to profit from that was to farm it, which was already being done.

None of it made any sense.

The scent of smoke caught his nostrils, and his head turned toward the smell. It was coming from across the field, beyond the trees.

He ran quickly across the fields, staying as low as he could. There wasn't an inconspicuous way to get to the tree line between this farm and the O'Leary's, so he just had to hope nobody was just inside the trees aiming at him right now.

Thomas made it to the trees without incident, the smell of smoke growing with each step. He could see it now, a haze in the air. He could also hear horses.

He moved as quickly as he could without sacrificing stealth as he approached the sound. What he saw as he came to the far edge of the trees made his blood run cold.

A group of men, easily two dozen, milled about some distance out from the edge of the O'Leary's fields, which were ablaze. The wheat had caught like dry tinder, and the fire was spreading fast.

The men were, as he'd figured, white men, and the only native clothing in sight was the moccasins on every foot. They were rough moccasins, not Tsawi design at all, but one of the men held a quiver of Tsawi arrows.

He wondered for a moment why they hadn't troubled the Briggs's farm, as they'd already attacked the O'Leary's, but realized almost immediately that the condition of the fields and lands around the old farmhouse probably made them think the place was still uninhabited and not worth the trouble. Thank God, he thought.

The men's horses were uneasy by the proximity to the fire, and nickered and pulled nervously, but the men held them fast.

"All right, let's get out of here before these fine folk come out to watch their crops burn," laughed a voice. The voice was met with more laughter, and a few poor attempts at tribal war cries.

As the men mounted and began to turn, he saw some of their faces. One of those faces he knew, and the recognition sent a jolt of shock through him so profound that his knees nearly buckled.

That face turned suddenly to stare straight in his direction. Thomas ducked back deeper into cover. All the other men sensed the first's hesitation and turned to see where the first was looking.

Memories of a childhood of death, violence, and cruelty raced through his mind before giving way to equally painful, more recent memories. All of this burned in a flash in his mind. And then the man whistled, gesturing for the men to ride out. The men followed his order, and he turned his horse to go.

Thomas stared in complete shock, the blood draining from his face. His breath seized in his lungs, but his heart pounded in his chest like a blacksmith's hammer.

It was impossible. That man had gone way out west many years ago, and the last Thomas had heard, he was dead. He'd been hanged for his crimes somewhere in Nevada.

Except he clearly hadn't.

Jonathan Jarrett, Thomas's older brother, was alive.

Chapter Thirteen

"What are you doing?" Rue asked, coming into the church to see Reverend Jarrett sitting on one of the pews, just staring at the cross on the wall behind the altar.

He looked back slowly, like he was having trouble bringing his thoughts around to her presence.

"Good evening, Miss Briggs," he said softly, a faint smile brushing the corners of his lips before his eyes turned back to the cross.

Hesitantly, she moved toward him.

"May I sit?" she asked, gesturing to the bench beside him. He nodded. "You seem troubled. Is this about…" she stopped, unsure what to say about their encounter that morning. She should probably apologize.

"What?" he asked in confusion.

Then, clearly realizing what she meant, he quickly looked away. She could swear she saw a trace of color come into his cheeks. It was quite possibly the most unexpected, charming blush she'd ever seen.

"No, no, it isn't that," he assured her. "I… I learned something this afternoon, and I'm trying to understand it. And figure how to handle it."

"Do you want a listening ear? I've been told I'm a good listener," she told him. What she really wanted to do was hold him and comfort away his evident pain, but she would offer what she could.

"It's…" He paused and sighed. "I don't even know where to start or what I can say," he said hesitantly.

"You could start from the beginning," she suggested with a reassuring smile.

He looked at her again, and she could see the darkness in them even stronger than before, but more than that, she saw pain, confusion, and fear.

For a moment, she thought he was going to tell her. Then, she saw the resignation deep in his eyes, and he turned away.

"No, I can't. I'll tell you what I can, though. After we… I mean, when I left you at the spring this morning, I went out to your farm," he admitted.

Rue blinked in surprise.

"Really? Why?"

"I wanted to see if I could find more clues about what's going on."

"And…?" she pressed.

"And I know who's behind all of it. Or at least, who's been staging the Tsawi attacks."

"I beg your pardon?" she asked incredulously.

"You know what's going on, and you're sitting here? Why on earth aren't you talking to the sheriff?"

"I don't entirely know what's going on, or at least not why, but I know who and how. And I'm going to. I'll talk to him when he gets back from the O'Leary's farm."

"What's he doing out there?" she asked.

"Putting out the fire in their fields. There was another attack. I saw it and came back here as quickly as I could to get some men out there to stop the blaze. Their field is pretty close to their house. I don't think they'll be able to stop the field from burning to the ground, but they should be able to keep the house and surrounding grounds intact."

"Why aren't you out there helping?" she asked. He looked at her, eyes slightly hurt, and she held up a hand placatingly. "I'm not judging, just asking."

"I'm... shaken. I wouldn't have been much help."

"I don't understand, why would..." she froze as the truth occurred to her. "You know the person."

He nodded slowly.

"And they're someone that means something to you," she added.

He nodded again, eyes closing for a moment.

They were both quiet as she processed this. Someone he knew and cared about was behind all of this. Was it because someone was trying to hurt him? Or was it one of life's all-too-frequent, all-too-painful coincidences?

"You're going to tell the sheriff, right?" she asked softly. He nodded once more.

"Of course. It's just…" Reverend Jarrett glanced at her again, and she saw the fear again.

"Just what?" she urged. He so obviously wanted to tell her, but for some reason, he was afraid of her reaction to it.

"Everything I love, excepting only God, is in jeopardy right now. I have to tell Sheriff Rawlins. I have to. But it will cost me dearly to confess it."

"You can confess to me, if you like," she said, smiling. He gave her a wry grin.

"You're not a priest and aren't bound by the sanctity of the confessional," he pointed out.

"Still, you wouldn't be the first man to confess his secrets to me. If it'll help you to say them out loud before talking to the sheriff, I'm an excellent confidante. If it won't help, I won't press."

Reverend Jarrett sighed deeply, a sound of profound loss.

Rue looked into his stunningly beautiful, captivating eyes as he turned toward her, and watched the swirl of emotions hidden beyond the gray. There was a vulnerability there she suspected nobody ever saw. Ever. She was powerfully, deeply touched that he would show it to her now.

"The men attacking the farms aren't the Tsawi. They're white men. They're attacking the farms, killed Mr. Dalton, and are leaving evidence that points to the Tsawi. We knew all of this already. I haven't figured out why they're doing it, but I saw them riding out after setting the O'Leary's field ablaze. The man leading them is… I know him. He's a mercenary. A thief and killer of the worst sort. He won't hesitate to take a life, or a hundred, commit any act of treachery or cruelty, if it means getting paid."

Rue considered this. It made sense. All of it except why they were doing such things here.

"I can't imagine any reason to do such horrible things," she said. He shrugged.

"If the man I saw is involved, I guarantee you there's money in it. This isn't his usual pattern when he's acting on his own. He and his gang have been hired to do this, but I don't know why or by whom."

"Who is he?" she asked. He paused for a very long moment, then shook his head.

"That's for the sheriff."

"I understand. Would you like me to leave?"

"No," he said quickly, sharply.

Her heart fluttered at the quickness of his response.

"All right," Rue replied.

"But…" once more, he hesitated. His frequent pauses spoke more of his uncertainty in all of this than anything he could possibly have said out loud.

Rue didn't speak, she just waited for him to say what he wanted to say.

"Would you come with me?" he finally asked.

"Not inside, just… walk with me? I find that speaking to you gives me resolve."

Touched once more, Rue stood with a gentle smile.

"Of course. Come along, reverend. Time to battle some demons."

The look that flashed across his face was frightening and would have been downright terrifying if she hadn't known beyond shadow of a doubt that it wasn't meant for her. Her words had triggered something in him.

"Truer words than you could possibly know, Miss Briggs. A battle against demons this shall be, in more ways than one."

He stood with the slow, graceful movements of a large hunting cat. The reluctance in his eyes was gone. All that was left was steel and fire. This was the man behind the priest. This was the hardness he hid behind his easy smile.

As she looked into those dangerous eyes, however, she knew without question that the darkness there was not evil. Perhaps it may have been, once, but what she saw now in this good reverend was a willingness to fight tooth and nail for what he believed was right, with every last raging breath in his body.

This was a man to make the devil himself quake.

He boldly offered her his arm, which she took without hesitation. This was not a man to be feared when at his side, but God help anyone in his way.

Rue's hand warmed when she touched his arm, and not all of it was from his body's heat.

They walked briskly, but to her surprise, he spoke while they walked. His eyes stared determinedly straight ahead, as if they could conjure his destination by mere force of will. She wasn't entirely sure those eyes couldn't do exactly that.

"Miss Briggs, a lot of things are going to change for me, and for the congregation, after my conversation with the sheriff. Before all of that boils to the surface, however, I want to tell you how much it means to me that you and your family have come here to Granada. You've been a most welcome addition."

"Thank you kindly, reverend," she said simply, suspecting he had more to say. She didn't have to wait long.

"Beyond that, your kindness has been a huge boon to me in an unexpectedly dark time. This is a good town, full of good folk. Truly good folk. They don't deserve what's happening. I don't believe I'm to blame at all for his presence here, I doubt he even knows I'm here, but if I don't help do something about it, the sin will be equally mine.

"When you folks came, I saw an opportunity to bring another good family into the fold. You're quite the puzzle, though. Good heart, Christian family, but you don't seem too keen on the church. There's a past there, Miss Briggs. I see yours as well as you see mine."

Her breath caught at this admission. He knew she could see through the preacher and saw the darker man beneath. And he'd seen through her, as well, as she'd known he could.

More than anything, the past half hour had convinced her that he wasn't an evil man. The priest wasn't a façade, it was a new life. Much as her own new life wasn't a façade. But it wasn't who she'd been, either.

"I don't rightly know what your history is, Miss Briggs, and fairly, it ain't none of my business. But I wanted to tell you that here, it doesn't matter. Your good heart shows, and I believe if you're honest with them, the people here will respect that. Don't spend your time here shutting people out for fear they might discover who you were. As I've just learned the hard way, the past never stays in the past.

"Anyway, that's about all I had to say. Thank you again for your kindness, Miss Briggs, and I hope that you'll find happiness here."

"That sounds awfully final, Reverend Jarrett," she said, concerned.

"I do believe it is, Miss Briggs. However the next few days play out, I doubt I'll still be welcome here by the time all's said and done."

"Now that's just nonsense," she admonished, giving his arm a squeeze where she held it. "The people here adore you. I've heard more than one person tell us that you were a true godsend when

when at his side, but God help anyone in his way.

Rue's hand warmed when she touched his arm, and not all of it was from his body's heat.

They walked briskly, but to her surprise, he spoke while they walked. His eyes stared determinedly straight ahead, as if they could conjure his destination by mere force of will. She wasn't entirely sure those eyes couldn't do exactly that.

"Miss Briggs, a lot of things are going to change for me, and for the congregation, after my conversation with the sheriff. Before all of that boils to the surface, however, I want to tell you how much it means to me that you and your family have come here to Granada. You've been a most welcome addition."

"Thank you kindly, reverend," she said simply, suspecting he had more to say. She didn't have to wait long.

"Beyond that, your kindness has been a huge boon to me in an unexpectedly dark time. This is a good town, full of good folk. Truly good folk. They don't deserve what's happening. I don't believe I'm to blame at all for his presence here, I doubt he even knows I'm here, but if I don't help do something about it, the sin will be equally mine.

"When you folks came, I saw an opportunity to bring another good family into the fold. You're quite the puzzle, though. Good heart, Christian family, but you don't seem too keen on the church. There's a past there, Miss Briggs. I see yours as well as you see mine."

Her breath caught at this admission. He knew she could see through the preacher and saw the darker man beneath. And he'd seen through her, as well, as she'd known he could.

More than anything, the past half hour had convinced her that he wasn't an evil man. The priest wasn't a façade, it was a new life. Much as her own new life wasn't a façade. But it wasn't who she'd been, either.

"I don't rightly know what your history is, Miss Briggs, and fairly, it ain't none of my business. But I wanted to tell you that here, it doesn't matter. Your good heart shows, and I believe if you're honest with them, the people here will respect that. Don't spend your time here shutting people out for fear they might discover who you were. As I've just learned the hard way, the past never stays in the past.

"Anyway, that's about all I had to say. Thank you again for your kindness, Miss Briggs, and I hope that you'll find happiness here."

"That sounds awfully final, Reverend Jarrett," she said, concerned.

"I do believe it is, Miss Briggs. However the next few days play out, I doubt I'll still be welcome here by the time all's said and done."

"Now that's just nonsense," she admonished, giving his arm a squeeze where she held it. "The people here adore you. I've heard more than one person tell us that you were a true godsend when you came. A man not only of God, but of love. Which I always thought ought to be the same thing, but that sure doesn't seem to be the case a lot of the time."

"Kind of you to share that," he said softly. "It means a lot to know my time here has been a help to these folk."

"A great deal, to hear tell of it," she assured him. "I've no doubt that whatever your past, you're a good man. The people here know that. It'll all work out, you'll see."

"You've got a real gift for inspiring hope in a man. It's a pity you couldn't join the priesthood, Miss Briggs," he chuckled. She laughed out loud and was gratified to see a smile cross his somber face.

"Well now, wouldn't that be something? We'd certainly make quite the pair, you and I."

She blushed as she realized she'd just referred to them as a pair and was profoundly grateful his gaze never strayed from his goal.

He chuckled again, a sound that warmed her through to the soul. She could happily listen to that sound all day, she admitted to herself.

"Yes, ma'am. It might be inappropriate to say this, Miss Briggs, but I'm about to confess my darkest secret to the sheriff, so one more secret won't be the nail in my coffin." He paused a moment before continuing. "In any case, I find myself wishing that we hadn't met last week."

Rue frowned in confusion, trying not to feel

slightly stung by the words. That was a peculiar thing to say.

"And why is that, reverend?" she asked, tone cooling slightly. He must have caught her tone, because he looked her way for the first time since leaving the church.

"I sincerely apologize, Miss Briggs. I phrased that poorly. I only meant that I wish we had met at a different time in our lives. A handful of years ago, perhaps. A lot of things might have been different. Maybe for both of us."

She considered this for a moment before remembering that he hadn't been a priest all that long. He was admitting he might have tried to court her had they met a few years back.

The idea caused a surge of emotions in her. A girlish excitement that he was clearly stating that he was interested, followed by frustration that nothing could come of it, and that he seemed to be acting like he was walking to the gallows as they approached the sheriff's office.

She had already known that he must be attracted to her. Their encounter at the spring that morning had been ample testament of that. But hearing him outright admit it was a different matter.

"Reverend Jarrett, I do believe you're flirting with me," she teased.

He grinned. It was different than it had been, and it didn't make the hard edge behind his eyes fade as his smiles usually did, but it was genuine all the same.

"Why, that's absurd, Miss Briggs," he replied in a playfully lofty tone. "I'm an ordained minister of the church. We don't flirt."

"Oh, I see," she replied sagely. "I forget that all priests are immune to the vices of the common man."

He laughed, and her skin tingled.

"If only that were true, Miss Briggs. Most of us just try the best we can."

"Likewise," she replied sincerely.

For so long, she'd felt trapped by the world, forced into a life in a brothel. Once there, there seemed to be no escape. And with her separation from her family, she had nobody to turn to try and break free of the chains she'd locked around her own wrists. She'd felt forced into it, but she'd made the decision. In the end, she couldn't help but feel partly responsible for her predicament.

But then, Josie's husband Mark had passed away, and she'd received that letter from her sister, and everything had changed. Here was family, a new home, a new start, a new chance. Everything she thought she'd never see again.

Then, she'd met this man. She didn't want anything to do with this priest. Except that she did.

Desperately.

He could understand her situation better than any, as he too had come from a dark life and tried to forge a better one for himself. She didn't know the details, but she didn't really need to.

Beyond that, something about him seemed to pull her in like a lodestone. She couldn't seem to stop her mind from moving his direction, her eyes from moving his direction…

That's quite enough of that, Rue, she firmly told herself in what had become very nearly a mantra. He stopped walking, shaking her out of her thoughts. They had arrived. The sheriff's door was open, and she could see him inside.

"Thank you again, Miss Briggs, for your kindness and company. There's no need to wait, I may not be coming out for a long while."

Something about the way he said that sent a chill up her spine. It sounded like a goodbye.

In a gesture she hadn't seen in many years, he reached down and took her hand, bowing over it as he gently brushed his lips across her skin. The chill in her body was instantly replaced with a flush of heat.

"Goodbye, Miss Briggs," he said, then turned and walked inside the sheriff's office, closing the door soundly behind him.

No, she thought as the dull thud of the closing door caused her to start and an unexpected lump to form in her throat, *that* was a goodbye.

Chapter Fourteen

The closing of the door behind him felt so final. Thomas took a moment to collect a breath before stepping toward the sheriff's desk. He was deep in paperwork, as Thomas had expected the man to be.

"Sheriff Rawlins?" he started, pleased with how steady his voice sounded. Inside, he wanted to scream, rail, to do anything but admit what he was about to admit.

The sheriff looked up, smiling wearily at Thomas as he saw him.

"Hello, reverend. I appreciate that tip about the field fire. We kept it from spreading, but that field won't have much of a crop this year. We'll all chip in to help them out, though, right, reverend?"

"The community absolutely will rally around, sheriff. They always do."

The sheriff, a keen-minded man, immediately focused more sharply on Thomas.

"They?" he asked. "Something I need to know, reverend?"

Thomas took a deep breath and nodded.

"Yes, sir, I'm afraid there is."

The sheriff simply gestured to the chair on the other side of the desk. Thomas sat.

"I have further information you'll need to know," Thomas said. The sheriff nodded for him to go on.

Well, enough procrastination, Thomas told himself. Time to bite the bullet. Perhaps literally.

"The perpetrators of all of these crimes is a gang of mercenaries, sir. Brutal and cutthroat, worst of the breed. The good news is that it isn't the Tsawi, which we'd already figured. The bad news is that these boys are much, much worse."

"You're talking like you know 'em, reverend."

"Just one of them, sheriff. Their leader." He took a steadying breath, his next words tumbling out in a rush. "My brother, Jonathan Jarrett."

Thomas braced for the explosion. The yelling, the panic, the reaching for the gun, all the expected reaction to admitting to a sheriff that he was a retired killer on the run. There was none of that. Any of it. Sheriff Rawlins looked mildly surprised, but that was it.

"That so? I'd heard he was caught and hanged in Nevada some years back," was all he said.

"That's what I'd heard, too."

"Have you talked to him?"

"No, sheriff. I saw him from a distance. I'm not sure if he saw me or not. If he did, things are going to get a whole lot worse very quickly."

"We'll be needing to call in some help from Kansas City, if it's the Jarrett Gang."

"Yes, sir," Thomas said, hesitantly. This wasn't going at all the way he expected it to.

"I appreciate your bringing this to me, reverend. I'll send a message off to Kansas City. They'll send some men and let the U.S. Marshals know the situation. Thank you, reverend. I'll take care of it."

"Sheriff?" Thomas asked, more unsure in this moment than he ever had been before in his life.

"Yes?"

"You don't seem to really... understand the situation."

"What, you don't think he's here because of you, do you?" the sheriff asked, frowning.

"No, sir, I don't, but..."

"I'm well acquainted with Jonathan Jarrett's history, reverend. I know how dangerous he is. Don't worry, I'm not going to take this situation lightly. Not by a long shot."

"I'm Thomas Jarrett," Thomas tried slowly, wondering if the old sheriff were perhaps going senile. If he were that familiar with Jonathan's history, he had to be even more familiar with Thomas's own.

"Yes, sir, I'm aware of that fact," the sheriff said, a bit of a sparkle in his eye.

"Jonathan Jarrett's brother?" Thomas tried one last time.

SAINT'S PRAYER

Sheriff Rawlins leaned forward, putting his elbows on the desk and steepling his fingers as he gazed intently at Thomas. No, Thomas corrected himself, this man was not senile. Not at all. The mind behind those steady eyes was still sharp as the barber's razor.

"Reverend, if you're trying to tell me who you used to be, I already know all about you."

Thomas was glad he was sitting down already. He might have fallen over had he been standing. The sheriff already knew? How? Why hadn't he done anything about it?

"You already..." He took a breath and tried again. "Sheriff, I'm afraid I'm a tad confused."

"Boy, you must have been plucked from the vine yesterday if you think a sheriff in this part of the country wouldn't recognize the name of Thomas Jarrett. More than that, I've seen your wanted posters a thousand times and would have recognized you from fifty yards out. I burned every one I could find the day after you rode into town. I know full well who you are, and I have since I first laid eyes on that rough-looking face of yours."

"Then what... why?" Thomas stuttered out.

"Because if I know two things in this world, it's that a gunfighter without a gun isn't looking for trouble, he's looking to hide. And that a man looking to hide is either hiding from the law or hiding from his past. In neither case is that man liable to raise much of a ruckus in a sleepy little town like this one so close to the big city. Not in the first few days, at any rate. Trouble is more likely to come from outside than in, in that case.

"Those first few days, I did some research. Sent some messages out, called in a few favors, and do you know what I learned?"

"What did you learn?" Thomas asked weakly, trying to digest this unexpected turn of events.

"I learned you really had gone to the seminary and had actually spent the last few years studying and becoming ordained. Care to reckon what that told me?"

"I can't imagine," Thomas replied in awe.

"That you were definitely looking to hide, not cause trouble. And from your past, not the law. If you were looking to hide from the law, you'd have used a false name. Not that it would've helped you, since I recognized you anyway."

"So why say nothing? Why not turn me in? There's still a respectable bounty on my head, if I'm not mistaken. And a man with my background could just as easily turn and start killing again."

"I believe a man deserves forgiveness just as much as he deserves justice, if his heart has turned away from his wrongdoing. If you meant my people harm, I'd have done my slap best to put a bullet between your eyes, and don't you doubt that for a second.

"But all signs pointed to you trying to change your life for the better and do some good for other folk in the process. Son, I'm all for that. Done a few things myself I ain't proud of. Nothing like your record, mind, but bad enough.

"I watched you like a hawk for months, and kept my ears open for word from outside that you'd been involved in something shady recently. But you, sir, are a blessed fine preacher, and this town hasn't seen better since it was formed.

"You've done a lot of good for this community in the last two years, reverend, and I respect that more than I can say. Whatever you were before, you're a good man now. And the last thing this country needs is more good men behind bars."

"I don't know what to say, sheriff," Thomas said sincerely, feeling choked up for the first time since he was a kid.

The fact that this man of the law had known who he was, from the very first day, and freely granted the second chance so desperately desired was a miracle of nearly biblical proportions. And for it to be granted to someone like him? He truly had no words.

"No need to say anything," Sheriff Rawlins said gruffly. "A man deserves a second chance if he's willing to earn it. You've earned it."

"Thank you," Thomas said softly, not trusting his voice not to crack.

He stood, and the sheriff did, too. Thomas held out his hand, and the man stepped around the desk, took it firmly, and gave it a solid shake. Unable to resist, Thomas pulled him in for a hug. There was a moment of surprised resistance, then a laugh as the sheriff returned it briefly before pulling away.

"All right, that's enough of that. Go take care of your flock, reverend. I'll do the same."

"Yes, sir. Thank you."

"Get," the sheriff said gruffly, but with a smile twinkling beneath his gray moustache.

Thomas walked out the door with a lightness in his head that was nearly euphoric.

He knew she wouldn't be there, but he couldn't stop a pang of disappointment when he saw she'd gone like he'd told her she should.

That situation was a whole different passel of coons, he knew. There was impossible, and then there was impossible. The worst part about it was that she seemed at least somewhat inclined his way. But his calling to the church forbade it, even if his brother's arrival hadn't put the nail in his proverbial coffin.

Potentially his literal coffin, too, he thought, despite his miraculous salvation from the hangman's noose. If Thomas got in his way, Jon might actually pull the trigger on him. Thomas wasn't sure, and that bothered him for more reasons than he could express.

The sheriff had said help was coming. Thomas worried, though, that help wouldn't come in time. Things were going to escalate. He suspected that Jon's end goal was the ruination of the town, in any way he could bring that about. Why, Thomas had no idea, except that he was being well paid to do it. Framing the Tsawi had a lot of potential, but the town was still holding strong, in part thanks to Thomas's continued calm reassurances, so Jonathan would escalate until he got results.

If all else failed, Thomas wouldn't put it past him to simply ride through the town with the whole gang gunning down every man, woman, and child they could find. That couldn't be allowed to happen. Jonathan needed to be stopped.

It was a frustrating dilemma that his knowledge of who was committing these crimes was helpful, allowing them to be more prepared and not underestimate the enemy, but if Jonathan found out that Thomas was here right now, in this town…

Well, a full-scale massacre was far more likely, in that case. Jonathan wouldn't risk the potential damage Thomas could inflict on his plan. The only man more dangerous in the old Jarrett Gang than Jonathan was Thomas himself, and Jonathan knew it.

So much hinged on the unknown of whether Jonathan had seen him. Too much. And on whether Jonathan knew he'd joined the priesthood.

He couldn't risk it, he knew. He had to go try to deal with the situation himself. Help may not arrive in time, and even if it did, if they didn't bring at least a hundred men, Jonathan's crew would grind them up like sausage.

Jonathan didn't surround himself with weak or unskilled men. These weren't the usual barroom scum looking for a buck. If they rode with Jon Jarrett, they were killers of the first order. Sending a standard posse against them would be like throwing a kitten into a dogfighting ring.

The trouble was, he had no idea if it was even possible to stop men like this without a gun; and a lot of them, preferably. But guns were something he'd sworn off when he took on the mantle of a priest. Men like this only stopped when they were dead. And, in Jonathan's case, it seemed sometimes not even then.

He could try to talk to Jonathan. Jonathan wouldn't shoot him, he knew that much. There was still love between them, though Jonathan was doubtless bitter about Thomas's leaving. If Thomas drew on him, Jonathan would shoot back, but it was the only imaginable case where Thomas himself would be a target.

The gang wouldn't be likely to shoot an unarmed priest, either. At least, not without Jonathan's order. Which would doubtless come, if that priest weren't Thomas himself.

If the US Marshals were already on the way, or if Jonathan thought they were, it might be enough to dissuade him from continuing the job, since completion would be significantly more difficult. Unless the pay was high enough, in which case, his talking to Jonathan would trigger a full-town massacre in hopes of their getting the job done and leaving the area before the marshals arrived.

Thomas sighed sharply in frustration. There were no easy answers. God would have to provide the solution, he knew.

As always, there was no other way.

Chapter Fifteen

The church rang with the sounds of the playing children back in the rectory. It was a happy sound that Thomas wasn't accustomed to, and it made him smile.

He stepped into the rectory and was greeted by a sharp, excited increase of shrieks and laughter from the children. In seconds, he was swarmed by tiny people, tugging at his clothes and dragging him further into the room.

Thomas laughingly went along with it, allowing himself to be led across the room and forced into a chair. Two of the children held him there while the others pretended to tie him down, arms 'bound' to the chair.

He looked up, grinning, and met Rue's eyes, gazing back at him with a warm, surprised smile. She hadn't expected to see him. In fairness, he hadn't rightly expected to be seen, either.

Thomas couldn't stop his own smile changing in tone. Maybe imperceptibly, but he felt the difference and it struck him.

Turning his attention back to the children, he put on an expression of effrontery.

"Now, children, I must protest! What in the world have I done to warrant such imprisonment?"

The children laughed, and he was pleased to see Robbie and Marshall both laughing and playing right along with the little ones. They'd been through a lot, he knew, and seeing them opening up like this, being the children they were, even if only for a moment...

It brought his heart joy. And steeled his resolve for what he had to do. But not yet. For a moment, at least, maybe his last chance, he could enjoy a few breaths of peace and happiness.

"You're a bank robber!" Robbie explained.

"Am I now? And I suppose that makes you the marshals?" Thomas assumed.

"No, just he's Marshall," protested little Mark, his three-year-old grasp of the language clipping the sentence in a fashion that made Thomas chuckle.

"Oh, of course. How silly of me!" he replied.

"Now we're arresting you. You're going to be in jail forever!" Lucy told him with a giggle.

"Never!"

Thomas roared suddenly, pretending to break his bonds with a mighty surge and leaping to his feet with a snarl. The children shrieked and ran, the group of them creating a swarm of chaos in the small room.

Chasing the children around, he pretended to just barely catch hold of one after another, letting each break free in their frantic surge of excited panic.

Marshall and Robbie leapt on his legs, causing him to trip. He controlled his fall carefully, making sure not to land on any of the other children.

"No!" he protested as the kids quickly piled atop him, holding him desperately to the floor. "You can't! I'm the best bank robber in the world! I must escape!"

"You can't!" Robbie argued. "This time, we're using chains. You can't break them!"

"Curses!" Thomas laughed, eyes turning from his awkward position on the floor to look up at Josie and Rue.

Both were laughing, but it was Rue's laugh that warmed him through to his soul. And her eyes, filled with a complex cocktail of emotions he couldn't entirely sort out. But he could see enough of it to bring a rising ache into his chest.

"I'm sorry, children, but I'm afraid I must go," he said with a sigh after another moment's mock-futile struggling against his imaginary iron bonds. It was time, and he couldn't postpone any longer.

"You can't!" Robbie said again, hands on his hips as he stood and loomed over Thomas. "You're arrested!"

"I have to be transferred to a big prison in Kansas City. Can't hold big criminals long-term here in Granada," Thomas reasoned.

"He's got a point," Marshall agreed reluctantly.

He stood, and the younger children did, too.

Thomas gave Marshall a grateful smile. Marshall gave him a smile and a nod. That boy would make a wonderful man, Thomas knew. His loving family had a lot to do with it.

Thomas wondered as he stood what it would be like to grow up in a family like that. He himself wouldn't have survived had it not been for his brother. There was love there, but it had been tempered in fear and pain, not joy and laughter.

The strength a man like Marshall would bring into the world was quite different from the strength Thomas himself had developed, but no less powerful for all that.

As he moved into the bedroom, the children returning to whatever game they'd been playing before the bank robber had invaded their den. It took him a moment to realize Rue had followed him. She leaned in the doorway in a casual pose, but he could read a hundred questions in her eyes.

"It didn't go the way you thought it would?" was the one she chose to give voice to.

"It most certainly didn't," Thomas said sincerely.

"You running?" she asked.

He paused a moment, unsure what she meant. Then it clicked in his mind. She thought he'd confessed a multitude of sins to the sheriff and had to escape town now. He hadn't had to do much confessing, not really, and he didn't need to escape.

But she didn't know that. Rather than answer her, he felt an overwhelming need to know the answer to a question of his own.

"Would you stop me if I were?" he asked, stepping closer to her.

"No," she said immediately. He didn't reply, because she didn't seem quite finished. She watched him for what felt a long time, then shook her head. "No, I wouldn't stop you."

"Why not?" he asked. "You have no idea what I might have done."

"You wouldn't run away just to save yourself. You're no coward. If you were running, there'd be a good reason for it."

"You've got a lot of faith in me," Thomas said, unable to stop a small smile from breaking through his serious expression.

"I do," she agreed so sincerely that his smile faltered.

"No," he finally explained, unwilling to let this conversation keep following its thread. He could feel where it was leading, and it was to a place he wasn't allowed to go. He'd stepped forward again and hadn't even realized it. "I'm not running. The sheriff and I are all right. I just have to go bring back Widow Riley. If I know these mercenaries, and I do, they'll circle south for their next target, now that the eastern farms have been cleared. They've come back every day since they first left sign. Near as I can figure, Widow Riley's farm is next, and I want her as far from there as possible when they come."

"I'll come with you. We can take the wagon; it'll be easier on the widow than riding." she said with a soft smile.

Every fiber of his being screamed at him to say yes, but he felt the thrumming of his heart in his chest, a vibration like a swallow's wings on a windowpane of the church, and knew it was a truly terrible idea for them to spend that time alone together.

"I appreciate the offer, Miss Briggs, but I can get there faster on Lady," he replied. He could see her expression fall, and it almost physically hurt him.

"All right. But take the wagon anyway. I'm just trying to picture you carrying poor Widow Riley on the back of your horse, and it makes my tailbone ache for the old woman." Rue smiled, but Thomas could see she was hurt he didn't want her to come.

"She's got a wagon with a padded seat she prefers," he explained, "but it is very kind of you to offer."

Rue nodded and moved to turn away.

"Rue," he said, stopping her. She looked back. "I'm afraid they might not wait a day to come back," he told her.

It was one of several reasons it was a terrible idea for her to come with him, but it was also the easiest and safest to say out loud.

"I might get there to find… I don't know. They might still be there, or arrive while we're there, or…

I just can't be sure it's safe," he finished lamely. He looked down before looking back up for her response.

Rue considered him for a long moment. Long enough that he started to worry. Then a playful, teasing spark lit in her eyes that stoked the fire within his chest.

"No need to explain. I understand completely."

"You do?" he asked, quite certain he was not thinking the same thing she was.

"Of course," she said confidently. "You're trying to spend some time alone with Widow Riley. I can't blame you, really, she's a lovely woman, and with so much experience…"

She trailed off with a grin as Thomas broke into laughter. He shook his head wryly.

"You are an absolute terror," he chuckled.

"It's not my fault you're attracted to older women. And she is quite a woman. But I'll be honest, I suspect she won you over with her cookies," Rue said with a wink.

Thomas's grin felt like it couldn't get any wider, but he reined it in for a contemplative expression.

"They are the finest cookies this side of the Mississippi," he agreed, staring off into the distance thoughtfully. "Maybe the other side, too." Rue laughed and gave him a playful shove.

"Now don't you dare go breaking that lovely woman's heart, Jarrett," Rue admonished sternly, but the teasing light in her eyes was glittering brighter than ever.

His heart lurched at her use of his name without the title. She'd never spoken it before, and she didn't seem to notice she'd just done so.

He placed a hand solemnly over his chest and spoke in as serious a tone as he could muster.

"Madam, my days of breaking hearts has long since come to an end. I aim to see if I can make an honest woman out of Mrs. Riley."

Rue laughed hard, and it made Thomas laugh, too. Her laugh was infectious. It was so open and unabashed. So many women would titter coyly and hide their mouths behind their hand as they did so.

Not Rue.

Rue laughed loudly, openly, and with a total lack of shame. It was the most beautiful sound he'd ever heard in his life.

That thought sobered him, and he stepped back. Her warm, joyful gaze held his like his eyes had been fused in place. The fire in his chest was burning, almost smothering him with its urgency. He needed to go.

Thomas turned and grabbed his long coat from the coat rack. It had been unseasonably warm of late, but it was liable to be dark before he made it back, and the nights had been getting a little brisk. He'd felt it the night before, sleeping in the hammock. It wasn't bad, but enough to be uncomfortable if not properly clothed for it.

Turning back, Rue stepped back from the

doorway, but stood to one side and watched as he came past her. He smiled at her as he passed. She fell into step behind him through the narrow hallway, then opened the door for him when he reached the door outside.

The kids were still playing wildly but took no notice of Thomas and Rue. Josie was a different matter.

Thomas smiled and nodded as he passed her on the padded armchair, but her look as she regarded them was entirely too full of underlying meaning and suspicion for his liking. Too full by half.

Josie knew there was something between them, he was sure. He and Rue had an electricity between them that he felt quite powerfully. Someone as close as her sister was bound to sense it on some level.

It didn't matter, he knew. His priesthood forbade it. Even assuming she'd still want to be with him when she learned he'd spent years racking up a body count that would give even the hardest member of Jon's current gang serious pause at the idea of standing against him.

It was best that he resolve this issue with Jon's gang sooner rather than later so she could return home with her family, and he could work on maintaining his distance a little better than he had been. If he survived.

One way or another, he would deal with Jon. He had to, for everyone's sake. But not least his own.

As he rode away, he'd have sworn he felt Rue's eyes on him every step until he rounded the corner by the schoolhouse.

But he didn't look back.

He couldn't.

Chapter Sixteen

"What was that all about?" Josie asked quietly as Rue came and sat in the wooden chair beside her.

"What do you mean?" Rue asked, though she knew exactly what her sister meant. The tension between her and Jarrett was palpable.

Josie stared at her, a blend of incredulity and chastisement.

"All right, all right," Rue said bitterly. "You want to hear it? You want me to say it?"

"Yes," Josie said simply, rocking the baby in her arms.

"I'm attracted to him."

"There, was that so hard?"

Now it was Rue's turn to aim an incredulous stare at her sister. Her ire was rising, and she knew she was about to direct her frustrations at her undeserving sister, but she couldn't stop the rush of emotion from taking over.

"Please tell me you're joking," she almost spat. "You must have cotton in your head if you think anything about this is easy. Let me explain this in words you can understand, sister dear. He. Is. A. Priest. A priest, Josie! All those years and all those men and I finally meet one I could actually fall for, and he's a blasted priest! What am I supposed to do with that? Nothing. That's what. Not a confounded thing. I get to spend God knows how many years here with you and these kids pretending everything is fine, and all the while, I'm over here secretly mooning over the local preacher."

"I don't like to say this, Rue, but if you keep looking at him the way I just saw, it ain't going to be a secret much longer."

"My god, Josie! I can't do this!"

"Do what?" Josie asked, her expression suddenly concerned.

"Any of it! I can't spend years pretending not to be attracted to someone when I am. I can't spend years avoiding him in a town with a population smaller than the balance in our bank account. But I can't do anything about it, either! I can't live here pretending to be something I'm not the rest of my life."

"What are you pretending to be?" Josie asked.

"A normal person!" Rue hissed, trying not to be overheard by the playing children all around them. "I can't keep pretending that I belong here, with good, upstanding folk like these, acting like I'm just one of the happy townsfolk. Do you know what they would do if they knew? What he would do?"

Josie clearly didn't have to ask who she meant

by 'he'.

"I doubt they'd take it as hard as you think, Rue. Neither would he. And you do belong here. With us. With me. None of the rest of it matters. The town can hate us, for all I care, which they don't. I have you, and I have my kids. You have me, and you have the kids."

"It's not enough, Josie," Rue said softly. "I'll never have what you had with Mark. And God help me, I want it. But for a thousand reasons, I never will."

"You never know what's coming down the road, Rue. You know that. You can't make predictions like that."

"None of it matters," Rue said, leaning back and closing her eyes with a sigh. "Even the best of men wouldn't touch me after… after knowing who else had."

"You're making assumptions again, Rue," Josie chastised. "We need to spend more time worrying about what we're doing right now than about what might or might not happen down the road. We need to worry about getting back to our farm and getting those fields worked. We need to worry about getting prepared for the winter. We need to worry about what we're going to do now that Georgia has noticed boys."

That last brought Rue up short.

"Wait, what?" Rue asked. Josie grinned.

"Georgia met the farrier's son this morning.

We went for a little walk and crossed paths with them. He's a darling lad. Name of Ricky, or Rico, or something of that sort. Georgia is completely infatuated."

"Good lord, already?" Rue said. "I thought we had years yet before that became a problem."

"Right? I was dead sure that Robbie would be the first to fall," Josie said, fondly watching the boys wrestle on the floor.

Rue glanced at her in surprise.

"Not Marshall?"

Josie shook her head.

"No, Marshall is too serious. He's trying too hard to be the man of the house since we lost Mark to really become a man yet. But Robbie? He's so sweet and sensitive. He'll fall hard when he does."

Rue considered this and knew her sister was right. Mark's loss had hit their whole family hard, though they were all taking it with the strong, quiet resilience Josie was near-legendary for.

The littler ones cried sometimes for him, and she'd heard Robbie crying quietly in the night a few times. Marshall never shed a tear, but always got real quiet whenever his father was mentioned.

She hadn't thought about it this way before, but she ironically had almost the opposite problem that they all did. They'd lost a vital part of their family and were trying to cope with his loss. Rue had suddenly regained a vital part of her family, and six new ones she hadn't known existed, and was trying to cope with their gain.

It had shaken up her life in ways she'd never expected. Not only had it been the way out she'd always wanted, but it had warmed parts of her soul that had frozen many long years before.

Those places in her heart hurt with the ache of the thaw, and the subtle warmth creeping back in felt as though it was burning her sometimes, so unaccustomed to the warmth was she.

Perhaps her attraction for the reverend was nothing more than a reawakening of a long-dormant part of herself. Maybe it was simply an infatuation, no more or less than Georgia's was for the farrier's boy.

But maybe it wasn't.

Rue sighed and stood, stretching.

"I think I need some air. I'm going to go for a walk," she said.

"Stay close," Josie said, a trace of nervousness in her voice. This business with the attacks had spooked her badly, Rue knew.

"Don't worry, I'll just wander toward the general store, maybe get a sweet for the kids."

Josie nodded, and Rue wandered outside. The afternoon sun was warm enough to be almost uncomfortable, but only just. She walked down the road, lost in her thoughts.

She'd never expected to be in this situation. Any part of it, from her sister and the kids, to this town, to being attracted to the town's reverend, to the random attacks on their and neighboring farms.

Rue didn't think it was at all unreasonable that she had absolutely no idea what to do.

It was odd that she took some comfort in thinking that Jarrett didn't know what to do, either. She saw the struggle in his eyes when he looked at her. She saw the darkness in his own past threatening, as her own did sometimes, to surge up and drown him in his own memories.

She wanted to comfort him, to put her arms around him and just hold him, smelling that crisp, clean scent he always had. She'd never known a man who smelled so clean all the time.

Rue really just wanted to tell him they'd figure it all out together, but she knew she couldn't. He wasn't hers, couldn't be hers. She couldn't even be sure it was anything more than a passing attraction.

Too much was up in the air right now for her to even recognize her own emotions with any clarity.

She sighed in frustration.

"Well, now, that wasn't a happy sound," came a friendly, warm, elderly voice.

Rue glanced over to see Widow Riley standing nearby. She looked like she had been heading the opposite direction to Rue. Her expression was concerned, but friendly.

"Good afternoon, Mrs. Riley," Rue said. "I'm sorry, I'm just woolgathering."

"That was more than just an idle thoughts kind

of sigh, young lady."

Rue almost laughed at being called young lady. She wasn't old, not by a fair margin, but she was no yearling filly, either.

"Really, Mrs. Riley, it was nothing."

"Nonsense. Come on, sit with me. I need a rest anyway."

Mrs. Riley turned and shuffled over to sit in one of two chairs outside the barber shop. The other chair was occupied by the barber, taking a breather, but he stood, tipped his hat to Rue with a gesture toward the chair, and headed back inside.

Rue gave him a smile and a nod and took the offered seat.

"Tell me all about it, love," the old woman said.

Rue thought about dismissing it again, but something about the old woman was at once supportive and non-judgmental.

"I'm a bit lost," Rue said.

"You don't mean lost on the way to the couture, I'd wager," chuckled the widow.

"No, ma'am, I don't," Rue said with a smile. Another person in this town it was impossible to dislike, Rue thought. "I've come from the city, but not the best part of the city, if you take my meaning. I lived a long time alone, far from family that didn't rightly want me."

"Now, I can see with my own old eyes that ain't true," Widow Riley replied. "Your sister wants you. She loves you something fierce."

"Yes, ma'am, that she does. But we spent a lot of years apart. But now, I'm living with her in this lovely town, helping raise children I didn't birth, just the two of us and the children, and on a farm, of all places. Lord knows I have no experience whatsoever on a farm, but here I am."

"That would take a fair shake to get used to," Widow Riley agreed encouragingly. Her tone implied she knew there was more.

"And then with all this fright over the attacks on our side of town," she began, then froze, looking over directly at the widow. "Mrs. Riley, the Reverend Jarrett just rode out to collect you at your farm."

"Collect me?" Mrs. Riley laughed. "Sakes alive, he's about sixty years too late for that, darlin'!" Her laugh turned into a guffaw and Rue joined in, not half because she'd been making similar jokes with Jarrett earlier.

"I mean to keep you safe from the attacks," Rue clarified, still smiling.

"Me? Good heavens, why?" she asked.

"He thinks your farm might be the next target," Rue told her.

"I dare them to try," Mrs. Riley grinned fiercely. Rue couldn't help but notice that Mrs. Riley's vibrant eyes were completely at odds with the many wrinkles on her face. Those eyes belonged in the face of a mischievous young woman, not a woman of the widow's years.

"I have no doubt you'd give them a good set-to," Rue chuckled. "But you know how he is. Always looking out for everyone else."

"Darling, I know all too well. He's such a dear. A real gem. If he weren't so infernally young, I'd have put my cap in for him myself, I'll tell you what."

Rue stared.

"But… he's a priest," Rue said.

"So?" Mrs. Riley said simply. "He wouldn't be the first man to leave a priestly calling for love of a beautiful woman."

Rue thought about that. The widow was right, Thomas could leave the priesthood if he chose. He'd need to seek release from his superiors, she thought, but she didn't think they'd deny him. It wasn't unprecedented. But for her? Give up everything he loved, the God he chose to serve, everything?

She shook her head suddenly, sharply.

"No, I couldn't do that to him," she said, half to herself.

"You couldn't do what, dear?" the Widow Riley asked, then stilled, watching her.

It was the kind of stillness that nobody under the age of seventy even seemed capable of. The kind of stillness that, if you didn't know better, you'd swear meant they'd just up and died on you.

Rue was instantly uncomfortable, and more than a little embarrassed.

"Oh, honey," the older woman said tenderly after a moment, reaching over and putting a surprisingly warm, strong hand over Rue's on the arm of her chair.

"What?" Rue asked, unwilling to be so rude as to move the woman's hand, and really not wanting to, but knowing exactly where this was heading and not liking it one bit.

Josie was right. She was never going to keep this a secret for long.

"Now I know why the sigh. All the rest is right enough reason to be a bit lost, but that sigh was deeper. You love that boy."

"Love?" Rue asked incredulously. "Goodness, no. I doubt I'm even capable, and I barely know him besides. I just find myself noticing what a fine figure of a man he cuts. Nothing more."

"Oh, tosh," Mrs. Riley replied. "I know me a sigh o' love when I hear one, dear. You just keep on denying it, but we'll both know deep down that it's true. And really, you couldn't find a finer man in the county. Maybe not even the country."

"But he's a priest," Rue replied wryly.

In a perfect echo of word and tone from before, Widow Riley replied simply. "So?"

"He's had a hard life, Mrs. Riley," Rue explained. Mrs. Riley nodded her agreement. "He found the church as a road to redemption." Mrs. Riley simply nodded, her expression encouraging her to keep going. "He has dedicated his life to serving God to redeem himself?" Rue said almost as a question, as if begging the old woman to see her point. Mrs. Riley's smile spread.

"Ah, but there are so many ways to serve God."

"Well, I know that, but…"

"But nothing. Now, I ain't saying he has any inclination toward leaving the priesthood, or whether he fancies you or the like, I don't claim to know the least bit about that. I'm just saying that if there's love there, from the both of you, God won't mind."

"I'm pretty sure that's blasphemy," Rue protested with an embarrassed laugh.

"I doubt it, but it don't make no difference to me, honey," Mrs. Riley laughed in return. "If the good Lord chooses to send me to the fires down below, it'll be for much more interesting things than a dash of blasphemy here and there!"

"Mrs. Riley!" Rue laughingly protested.

"Oh, don't get all excited on me now, Miss Briggs. I'm only joshing you. Truth be told, I'm a good Christian, as these things go. I do my best, like any good Christian does. Besides, there ain't nothing blasphemous about saying God is in favor of love, if that love is real."

"I don't think that's what the Bible means," Rue said dryly.

"Now, really. Anyone who's really read the good book knows there are plenty of stories about folk doing all sorts of things for love. From stealing to killing, for love of man or woman, for love of country or people, even for love of God Himself, people have done a lot for love that would otherwise be frowned on. And guess what?"

"What?" Rue asked, baffled as to where the peculiar old woman was going with this.

"Every one of them that did it for love, I mean real love, not just lust or obsession or some such sinfulness, God forgave them their sins. And that's breaking actual commandments, not simply choosing to serve Him in a different way than in the priesthood. I ain't saying we should go running about doing bad things and saying it's for love, or that some things done for love aren't truly wrong, but motive means a lot. Anything done for love, really for love, isn't unforgiveable."

"Some would argue that point," Rue replied.

"Sure, they would! But I just dare them to show me where in the Bible that it says that love's a sin. Now, you might still be thinking it ain't love you're feeling. Maybe it is, maybe it ain't. I got my suspicions, but that truth is for you to discover for yourself. Just like it'll be for Reverend Jarrett to decide how he feels."

"The whole argument is probably pointless, Mrs. Riley," Rue argued. "The whole thing might just be some silly girl's fantasy."

"All I'm saying is that it's right silly to give up on the strawberries just because they're on the other side of the fence. There's always ways around, over, or under a fence. And sometimes, that way is as simple as asking permission to go through the gate."

"I think we'd better head on by the church," Rue said, desperately needing to change the subject. "When the reverend finds you're not at home, he'll come back to town, and you can talk with him then. I'll let you argue with him about whether or not you'll be heading back to your ranch."

"All right, dear. It'll be so nice to see your sister and those lovely children. Come along, let's buy them a few sweets before heading back."

Rue smiled, unwilling to think too much further about what the widow had said. She wouldn't ask Jarrett to give up his calling.

Not for her.

Not ever.

Chapter Seventeen

Something was wrong. Thomas could feel it before he ever reached Widow Riley's farm. He had no idea what it was that he felt, but he definitely felt it. So did Lady.

Her ears kept swiveling around, listening to the tall grass around them, but she focused mostly forward, just like he did. There was trouble near, and they were walking straight toward it.

Not the first time, he thought. Also not for the first time, he wished he had a gun in his hand. He shook the thought away and focused.

As they drew nearer the farm, his view was obstructed by a surprisingly large row of berry bushes between the roadway and the farmhouse. Luckily, that view obstructed both ways.

He brought Lady up short a few feet before they came into view of the farmhouse and dismounted. Crouching low, he glanced quickly around the edge of the bush. The farmhouse was quiet. The kind of quiet that felt like it was screaming.

The scent of the long grass and the berry bush were all that reached his nose. Well, he corrected himself, that and Lady.

She nudged him with her nose, as if sensing his thoughts on her. He patted her nose calmingly, whispered a few soothing words, and told her to stay put. Obediently, she didn't budge, but the look she gave him was not an appreciative one. He chuckled softly and ducked into the grass on the other side of the bushes.

He moved slowly, carefully, and silently. Storm-Chaser had taught him a lot about stalking, and he was better than many, but he wasn't Storm-Chaser's equal in such things. He wasn't even Santiago's equal in stealthy movement.

Santiago was almost as good as Storm-Chaser, though, he thought. The sniper had a knack for spotting the best vantage points for his work, and just as good a knack at getting into position undetected. Not that you'd ever guess it to look at him.

Thomas wondered how Santiago was doing. The thought of his old friend sent a pang of guilt and nostalgia through his heart. Another good man hurt by Thomas's temper and violence.

Last he'd heard, Santiago had recovered and settled down somewhere in the New Mexico territory. Thomas hoped he was doing well, and enjoying a nice, peaceful life. Santiago was never good at peace, but he deserved it, Thomas thought.

There was a soft, but distinctive crack of a twig not far from him. He froze, sharp eyes focused tightly in the direction of the sound.

He waited what felt forever until he saw movement. Someone else was stalking toward the farmhouse. Another few moments and he got a glimpse of his fellow sneak.

It was one of Jonathan's men. Thomas recognized him as the one who had been beside Jonathan when he'd seen them before.

In older days, he'd have stalked and killed the man, then search silently for his fellows, eliminating as many as possible before the real gunfight started.

This wasn't older days.

Thomas moved silently up behind the man, so close he could have touched him.

"Hey," he said sharply. The man spun, revolver in his hand whipping around to point toward Thomas.

Thomas's hand shot out like lightning, snatching the gun right out of the stunned mercenary's hand. Before the man could say or do anything else, Thomas stood up, revealing himself to all around who might be watching.

"Jonathan!" Thomas yelled.

The man in front of him stood slowly, staring at Thomas in complete astonishment. He glanced down at his gun in Thomas's hand.

Thomas didn't hold it like a weapon. He held it back out to the man. It was a risk, he knew, but a calculated one.

By calling out to Jonathan and then handing the gun back, he was attempting to establish he was a friend of Jonathan's, which he was not, rather than an enemy of the gang, which he was. But nobody here knew that. Except maybe Jonathan.

It was silent for nearly sixty seconds before heads began poking up all around the tall grass around the farmhouse. It looked like Jonathan had brought the whole crew to storm the farmhouse. A lot of effort for one little old lady, he thought. Though they'd have brought twice this many if they actually knew Widow Riley.

Another two dozen heartbeats passed before Jonathan himself stepped around the corner of the house, expression confused, and froze.

The brothers locked gazes; Thomas with determination, Jonathan with a mixture of surprise and a predatory satisfaction. Slowly, Jonathan walked toward him. Thomas walked forward as well, meeting his brother just inside the yard proper, where the grass had been trimmed back low.

"Tommy, Tommy…" Jonathan almost hissed. "I knew that was you."

"Jon," Thomas replied coolly.

"What in the Sam Hill are you doing out here? And dressed like a preacher? Ain't you afraid of being struck by lightning?" Jonathan said with a laugh. His cronies, who had begun crowding around, laughed with him.

"I am a preacher, Jon. Properly ordained by God."

His brother blinked, even more surprised than he had been a moment ago.

"Don't that just beat all," Jonathan said with a sneer. "Best killer in the country, and you've gone shepherd on me. You've spent too much time as a wolf to not want to eat a few sheep, little brother. Doing a little killing on the side?"

The men around Jonathan suddenly seemed to realize who Thomas was. Thomas Jarrett; myth, legend, killer. Thomas felt a touch of satisfaction as he saw the men almost as one move slightly further away from him, toward the concealing grass, whispering among themselves.

Good, he thought. Now they knew who they were dealing with. Or who he had been, at least. None of these men were in any danger right now, and if they drew down on him and decided to pull the trigger, he'd go down without a fight.

But he knew they wouldn't. Not a man among them would have drawn a gun on him purely because of his reputation, let alone because he was their boss's brother, and the boss hadn't drawn on him.

"No," Thomas replied. "I follow my vows. They're good folk here, Jonathan. They don't deserve this."

"Oh, please," Jonathan scoffed. "You think these folk don't beat up their kids? They don't lie, cheat, steal, and kill like the rest of us?"

"Nobody kills like you do, Jon."

"Gee, thanks, little brother. I'm gonna blush," Jonathan said with a mocking laugh.

Again, his cronies laughed, but it was a bit more subdued. They still eyed Thomas warily.

"What's the job?" Thomas asked.

"Pardon?"

"You heard me. What's the job?"

"You know," Jonathan said dismissively, "just shake things up a little and collect our payday."

"For whom?"

"Now, now, I ain't telling you that. Client confidentiality, little brother, you know that."

"Why here? Why this town? Why frame the Tsawi?"

"Come on, Tommy, you're smarter than that. Ain't you figured it out yet?"

"I'm afraid I haven't, Jon. Why don't you spell it out for me?"

"No. You gave up your right to know anything when you left me for those… Saints." Jonathan spat the word like a curse.

"You could have come with us, Jon."

"No, I couldn't."

Thomas sighed. "I know."

"Why are you here, little brother?"

"I told you, I'm a preacher now. This is my congregation."

"That ain't what I mean. I mean why are you

here, right now, talking to me. I thought it was you I saw the other day. I was expecting a fight. That's why we were so careful over here. Thought you might come by, irons hot, trying to play Saint with your boys. But this?" Jonathan gestured at Thomas in confusion, almost helplessly. He truly didn't understand why Thomas had come to talk.

"I told you, Jon. These are good folk. I don't know what you're doing here in this town, or for whom. All I know is that these people don't deserve this. They're not like the people we knew growing up, Jon. They're not like the people in your gang, or even like the people you're usually hired to work against. These are good, honest folk, who mean well and help each other out."

"Good, honest folk don't exist!" Jonathan yelled suddenly, his notoriously mercurial temper finally making an appearance.

"I didn't used to think so, either," Thomas agreed. "But I've met so many here. Don't do this, Jonathan. As your friend, as your brother, I'm begging you not to do this."

"The great Thomas Jarrett, begging for the lives of a bunch of farmers." Jonathan shook his head in disgust. "You were great, Tommy. A real legend. Grown men, U.S. Marshals, used to wet themselves when they saw you coming. Why would you walk away from that? Why become…" Jonathan gestured at the collar, disdain and puzzlement warring for dominance in his voice.

"I was tired of doing the devil's work for him," Thomas replied honestly.

"So now you do God's instead? What's the difference?" Jonathan asked.

"The difference is that now I help people instead of hurting them," Thomas replied. "People smile when they see me, they don't cry. They bring me plates of cookies instead of trying to put a bullet in me. It's really quite refreshing. You should try it," Thomas said dryly.

Jonathan leaned in close and almost whispered. "I like the sound of their screams, little brother. Don't you miss it?"

In his eyes, Thomas saw sincerity and a deep, unholy pleasure at the thought of making others suffer.

Thomas fought back the lump in his throat. His big brother, the boy he'd grown up worshipping, the big brother who'd taken beatings, and worse, to protect his little brother, truly was dead and gone. The man in front of him was a monster. And one that Thomas had already thought long buried.

In that moment, Thomas knew he had lost. There was no point in talking to Jonathan. He wasn't just doing this for money. He was doing it for the payday, sure, but he really did it because he enjoyed it. He reveled in the fear, the pain, the suffering of his fellow man. No demon of hell would have shown the glee at the idea of human suffering as Jonathan showed in that moment.

Without conscious direction, his mouth spoke the words in his mind. "You've become our father."

The fist came up fast and hard, slamming into Thomas's jaw with the force of a steam engine. Thomas had enough presence of mind to roll his chin with the punch, or Jonathan might have broken his jaw. As it was, Thomas wasn't sure he hadn't cracked a tooth or two. He felt blood swell in his mouth.

He turned his head coolly and spat, then looked back at Jonathan.

"I'm sorry, Jonathan," he said softly, but both knew he didn't mean about the remark.

Turning, Thomas walked toward the crowd of men. They parted in front of him uncertainly, glancing back at their leader for instruction.

They clearly got none, because the uncertainty never left their faces, and they parted to let him pass. More out of fear than anything else, Thomas knew. His legend parted an ocean of killers for him. Without contradictory instructions from someone they feared even more, in this case Jonathan, they weren't about to stand against him.

He walked back to where he'd left Lady, needing to go slowly enough that he'd know Jonathan's next move before he left. He didn't have to wait long.

The sound of whooping and shattering glass sounded behind him. He heard the rushing *whoosh* of alcohol igniting, and knew they'd thrown bottles of booze through the windows, followed by a torch or two.

There wasn't anything he could have done, he knew, and he'd seen Widow Riley's wagon was gone so knew she wasn't home, but still… Just climbing into the saddle and riding away felt *wrong*.

He could do nothing. Couldn't lift a finger to protect the people he cared about. Couldn't stand against the evil he'd rejected in any way beyond a weekly sermon to a half-asleep congregation.

Thomas was a fighter, not a pacifist, though he'd vowed to become one. He didn't want to fight anymore. But to not be able to even when he saw no other way to stop the flood of suffering evil wrought around him…

Good people were dying, and he did nothing. Could do nothing.

It was all so very wrong.

Even God needed warriors.

Chapter Eighteen

Rue walked the road toward the sheriff's office. She'd meant to ask Jarrett the night before for any updates, but he'd come in dark and upset, wanting only to talk to Widow Riley. They'd had a long conversation outside that she made it a point nobody in the house overheard.

Declining his invitation to stay at the church, the widow had already made arrangements to stay with her knitting circle friend, Mrs. Pomeroy, not far from the church. That was as much as Rue had heard later about their conversation.

When they'd come back inside, Jarrett had looked better, which had been a relief for Rue. He still looked upset, but nothing like when he'd walked in earlier. He hadn't spoken much the rest of the evening, just got a clean change of clothes, changed, and went to his hammock outside.

The brief moments he'd made eye contact with her had been potent and poignant. The looks spoke loudly that there was more he wished to say to her, but couldn't or wouldn't, for whatever reasons he might have. She suspected some of it, but knew she had no idea about the rest.

And she certainly wasn't going to pry. She respected his secrets every bit as much as he respected hers. He'd never once asked. Had never even mentioned it beyond the one time he'd admitted he knew she had some shadows in her past. And so, she returned the favor.

But that didn't mean she wouldn't pry with the sheriff to find out what was going on with the attacks.

As she opened the door to the sheriff's office, she didn't see anyone. She was about to call out to see if anyone was in one of the back rooms, but she heard voices.

Rue walked that way, but she froze when she heard Thomas's voice.

"…figure out how to stop my brother. He'll be back today, either to hit another farm, or to just ride through and sweep the town. How long until the marshals get here, sheriff?"

"It won't be until Thursday, at the…"

Rue hurried back out the way she'd come. It wasn't her place to overhear, and she wasn't a snoop. She'd heard too much already, she knew.

Thomas's brother…

That explained so much. And his brother might just raid the entire town? The idea was horrifying. The people here weren't afraid to fight, but she knew there was more than one man attacking the outlying farms. If he had enough men, they could kill every man, woman, and child in the entire town. And Thomas didn't seem to think that was out of the question.

She had to know more, but it wasn't her business. But it was her family she had to protect.

Besides, Thomas had the right to know what she'd overheard. He might be upset, but not as much as if he learned she'd overheard and didn't tell him.

Moving a little further down the street, she found a place to sit and watch, waiting for him to emerge. When he did, she stood and approached.

His smile when he saw her was warm, but weary. Even so, the way it lit up his face, and knowing that smile was for her, thrilled her no end.

"Morning, Miss Briggs," he said, tipping the brim of his hat her way as she fell into step beside him.

"I was coming to speak with the sheriff," she told him.

"I've just left him, now is likely a fine time to talk with him," the reverend told her. She hesitated, unsure how to approach this.

"Actually, now I need to talk with you more urgently."

Jarrett frowned and looked over at her, gray eyes attentive.

"Of course. Here?" he asked. She shook her head.

"Can we go someplace a bit more private?"

"The chapel is empty, will that do?"

Well, she thought, if there was a place for a confession, that would be it.

"That'll be just fine, reverend, thank you."

They walked in silence toward the church, and the reverend held the door open for her. Walking in, she sat in one of the pews, sliding over enough for him to sit beside her.

"I'm all ears," he said, sliding in beside her after taking a moment to pause and genuflect. She could still hear the caution in his voice, though.

"I was going to speak with the sheriff to ask how things were developing with the investigation into the attacks," she told him. He relaxed just enough for her to notice.

"Well, I can tell you we haven't learned much since last night," he started, but she touched his arm to stop him. He waited to let her continue.

"I went inside while you were speaking with him." At the sudden darkening of his expression, she hurried to clarify. "Now, the moment I heard your voice and realized the sheriff wasn't alone, I turned and walked straight back out again, but not before I heard something."

"What did you hear?" he asked quietly.

She couldn't quite identify the emotion in his voice. It might have been that he was upset she'd eavesdropped. It might have been a note of relief, though why, she couldn't have said.

"Not much, as I told you, I left the moment I heard your voice. All I heard was that… well, that it was your brother behind all of this. I'm not going to pry into any of it, it simply ain't my business, but I didn't want you to think I was spying or lying to you if you found out later that I'd heard as much, so I had to tell you."

Jarrett took a long, deep breath and sighed.

"That shows a lot of integrity," he said, sounding impressed. "In a way, I'm glad you heard."

"You are?" she asked, surprised.

"In a way," he repeated with a nod. "Secrets are hard to keep. It's a weight that drags on you, day in and day out. It was such a relief speaking to the sheriff."

"What I don't understand," she began, realizing his apparent intention to be forthcoming, "is why telling him the bandit is your brother would be dangerous for you."

Thomas hesitated, visibly steeled himself, then spoke.

"Jon and I used to ride together in a gang he led. I did a great many terrible things before I found my way out of his darkness."

Rue sat quietly and let that soak in. When she didn't reply, he continued in a sort of rush, as if he was afraid that if he didn't say it now, he never would.

"He looked out for me in a way nobody else ever did. Jon took more than a few blows meant for me. He was my older brother and would take a lashing, and sometimes worse, to keep me safe. I idolized him.

"Our father was a cruel and vicious man, and he beat the same into his children. Jon and I took the evil done to us and turned it around on others weaker than we were. Our targets got bigger as we did. By the time we were both men, he'd rallied quite a crew around us. We started doing the things we were already doing, but for money.

"From the time I was little, I followed my older brother around. He was my hero. When he turned to banditry, I didn't even hesitate. I followed him."

It explained so much, she realized. He and his brother had been raised by a cruel man and grew to be cruel men themselves. And yet, somehow, Thomas Jarrett had found his way out of that darkness, and had built himself a life of light.

It explained the steeliness and darkness in his gaze, but also the light and warmth. As she'd hoped, he was a man of virtue with a difficult and traumatic past. Mistakes had been made, but she could see he truly was a different man than he had been then. Somehow, having that confirmed made her even more drawn to him. She could relate on a level that most could not.

"How did you find your way out of that kind of life?" she asked softly.

"A very dear friend of mine practically dragged me out," Thomas chuckled. "It was a long, hard road back up, but between him and the rest of our group, they helped me make the climb. We turned vigilante, using our skills to catch men like those we'd once been. Protecting people, in our own way. The Saints of Laredo, we called ourselves. A bit high and mighty, I admit, but humility was never our strongest suit.

"Six men, some of the best, or rather worst, in the game. But six men trying to turn ourselves around and make a better world, and maybe buy back a little piece of their souls by giving of ourselves for others."

"What happened?" she asked him, captivated by the imagery his simple explanation was conjuring.

Not many men could walk away from a life of violence. She'd seen enough of that type to understand that quite clearly. To turn that into trying to help others was, while perhaps a little misguided, quite noble in its way. And a far cry better than what they had been doing.

"I had another fall, near the end," he explained, "and things didn't end well with us."

"I'm not sure I understand," she admitted.

He hesitated again, and she knew there was going to be another revelation in his next statement.

"One of our group, a man we called Kid Grady, won half the deed to a gold mine in a game of poker. The other half belonged, as we understood it, to a man wanted for bank robbery in half the territories of the United States. Kid wanted to go take it from him."

"And you didn't?" she encouraged.

"The mine was supposed to be a real motherlode," Jarrett told her. "Worth a fortune to anyone who owned the whole mine. But with the ownership split the way it was, neither could make legal move on the property without consent of the other. Which neither would give, of course. Stupid, since there'd have been more than enough to split and still make both very wealthy men.

"Kid Grady knew the man wouldn't give up or sell the claim. He argued that since the man was a crook, we'd go take him in and just take the deed as our reward. I argued that going after someone like that with intent to steal from him was a step back down the road we'd worked so hard to get away from."

"You were right," Rue said. It wasn't a clean moral dilemma, but she was certain Thomas had been on the right side of it. She wasn't sure how this constituted a fall for him.

"Yes, but I didn't say any of it well at the time. The argument escalated, and the others got involved. Jack and Storm-Chaser sided with me. Santiago and Lucky sided with Kid. Jack, in typical fashion, shoved Lucky when Lucky said a few unkind words to him. He was always a bit of a hothead, and far too quick with his fists.

"In response, Kid took a swing at Jack. Now, I'll tell you true, Jack's the best brawler I've ever seen. Ever. And I've seen more than a few. Kid Grady taking a swing at him was a bit like trying to take on a buffalo with a pellet gun. All it did was set Jack off. Santiago tried to step in and took a hit from Jack."

"The whole thing turned into a fist fight?" she asked in surprise, trying to picture the scenario he described. Jarrett shook his head.

"Lucky is a hothead. Even more so than Jack. When Jack turned on him after dropping Kid as if he really were nothing more than a child, Lucky drew his gun. I drew faster, as I always did, but Storm-Chaser grabbed my hand, and Santiago got in the way. I shot him."

Rue froze in horror. After a long moment, mouth going dry, she spoke. "But that was an accident," she protested, but starting to really understand the good reverend.

But Thomas shook his head, as she'd expected him to. She could see the course his mind had taken, and the guilt he still bore.

"Shooting Santiago was an accident, but I'd still meant to shoot one of my brothers."

"Did he…" she started, but trailed off, unable to finish the thought.

"No, he made it. Took the round in his left shoulder. Took the barber a bit of work to get the bullet out and stitch him up, and he had a fever for a few days, but he made it."

"Thank God," she breathed. Jarrett nodded his

agreement.

"I do. Every day. But I had to walk away. After that, Jack left. He was really the lynchpin for the Saints. Kind of our leader, though unofficially, and Grady would have argued the point. When he left, with the bad blood between the rest of them, they all just sort of drifted away."

"Jarett, I'm so sorry…" she said, forgetting his title altogether.

"Thomas," he replied, giving her a peculiarly shy sidelong glance.

"I beg your pardon?" she asked, confused by the sudden shift in him.

"You can call me Thomas. If you want to," he amended.

It was almost boyish, and she could see that his vulnerability, guilt, and pain over the story he was telling had opened other emotional doors, as well.

"Thomas," she said, tasting it on her tongue. Her nephew's name was Thomas, too, but it felt different on her lips when she said it as this man's name. "I'm so sorry, Thomas."

He nodded.

"I fell into a dark place again. I'd drawn blood before, but this was different. Santiago was my friend. More than my friend, he was my brother. To have hurt him was… Well, it was more than I could take. I about lost myself then, almost went back to my brother Jonathan."

"Why didn't you?" she asked.

"When a man has drawn so much pain, suffering, and blood out of his fellow man that he feels he's going to drown in it, out of desperation, he gives up his soul completely. Either to God, or the devil. I chose the former. Jonathan did not."

She nodded, nearly overwhelmed at what he had endured in his road to redemption.

"And so, I joined the seminary instead of rejoining Jon's gang."

"So, he's here to hurt you?" she asked uncertainly. Thomas immediately shook his head.

"No, he didn't know I was here until yesterday. I went and talked to him."

"You what?" she asked, horrified.

"I had to. If he's here, things have to be handled delicately. The sheriff can't handle this crew, all he can do is call in some help from the city, but I doubt it'll arrive out here in time to be of any use. Jon's boys have been coming back every day. I knew they'd hit Widow Riley's farm next, but after that? I'm not sure. Nowhere else is along that route. He'll circle to another part of town, especially since he knows I know it isn't the Tsawi. Framing them is pointless now."

"So, what will he do?"

"He'll escalate everything, and possibly shift plans to account for me."

"You think he'll ride through and butcher the town," she said, rather than asked. She'd heard enough of his conversation to know he'd been worried about just that.

"I don't know. He might. It's big, bigger than anything he's done before, and will call down heat from the marshals unlike anything he's ever known, but if the payday is enough…" Thomas trailed off.

He didn't need to finish the sentence. She knew what he meant.

"Did talking to him help at all?"

"No," Thomas said, voice eerily emotionless. "Any trace of hope I'd had at learning he was still alive died the moment I looked into his eyes yesterday. There's nothing human left in him. The brother I knew and loved, who protected me even from our own father, is gone."

"Thomas…" she started, but Rue had no idea where to go from there. She put her hand over his, squeezing it.

Her touch shifted something in him again, and she saw the pain he was holding back flood forward. He didn't weep. She wasn't sure a man with his past even could. But she could almost hear his soul crying out at the loss and pain he felt about his brother.

He leaned slightly toward her, sliding sideways along the back of the pew. Keeping her hand over his, she shifted position to put an arm around him.

Thomas's head came down to rest on her shoulder, and she held him close.

She had no idea how long they sat like that and didn't rightly care. He needed this, she could feel.

And truth be told, she did, too.

After a too-brief eternity, he pulled back and sighed.

"I'm sorry, Rue," he said.

She hadn't told him he could be so informal with her, but it didn't even occur to her to mind. The sound of her name on his lips grew a pleasant warmth deep within her.

"I gave up a lot for the church when I joined the priesthood," he continued. "It's been worth it. The redemption and opportunity to help others that I've found in God has brought a peace and joy to my soul I'd never even dreamed existed."

"I'm not sure why you're apologizing to me for that," she said, confused again. This conversation had been quite the emotional bronco ride already.

"Because…" Thomas hesitated, looking away before turning his gaze back to her. "Because I've gotten too close to you. It's not proper, and isn't my place, my position being what it is."

"I know, Thomas. Don't worry, I know. I wouldn't ask you to do anything other than to keep your vows close. I'm sorry, too. It's been a surprise, meeting you, and I haven't behaved properly, either. I know I'm not making it any easier on you."

"It's my fault, not yours," Thomas argued. "but either way, I need to step back. I need to focus on dealing with my brother, and then on helping my congregation cope with the loss of Mr. Dalton and the fears they've all been forced to endure at the hands of my brother and his crew. I just... I just can't, with…"

Thomas stood and shook his head.

"I'm sorry, Rue. I should go. I have to think. And I need to decide what I'm going to do about Jon."

"Of course," she said, standing as well.

To her astonishment, he leaned forward and gently kissed her cheek. His hand reached hers and gave it a squeeze before he let it fall once more, turned, and left the church.

This was a goodbye of a different sort entirely. This wasn't a goodbye that filled her with fear as his last had. This was a goodbye that tore into a place in her heart she didn't even know existed.

There was no hope for them. And if he confronted his brother, there may be no hope for him, either. But none of it was her decision. She wished desperately she could help him in this, but she was even more helpless than he was.

Rue sat back down in the pew and cast her eyes to the large, simple, elegant wooden cross hanging behind the altar, though she stared far, far beyond the symbol.

She barely noticed when the tears came.

Chapter Nineteen

Thomas walked aimlessly through the town. He had no idea where he was going, or what he was doing. He was having trouble focusing his thoughts in the chaotic tumult of his brain. He was facing more than one life-changing decision at this moment, though if the one went badly, the other would be moot.

He'd already made the decision on the second one, anyway. Thomas couldn't be with Rue. It was that simple. His heart might argue it, and did so quite aggressively, but he knew he couldn't. She deserved better than a former killer and current fallen priest, which he would be if he left his order for her.

It wasn't fair to her, wasn't fair to his congregation, and wasn't fair to Josie and the kids. He couldn't take Rue from them, either, and he didn't want to. They needed her, and she needed them. Taking her from them would be an act of cruelty.

It was absurd that the thought had even crossed

his mind. He barely knew her, really. There was just that irresistible draw he felt to her. That was all. That and her kindness. And sense of humor. And her compassion. And her wit. And…

Get it together, Thomas, he snapped at himself. You need to be focusing on Jonathan.

Jon was certain to strike again, and soon. And Thomas had no idea where. There were more outlying farms on the outskirts on the west side of town, but he didn't think Jon would ride the gang all the way around to hit the opposite side. It was too obvious.

Thomas wasn't convinced Jon would just massacre the whole town in a riotous attack, but he wasn't convinced he wouldn't, either.

If Jon did that, Thomas had no idea what he would do.

Or even could do.

He could hide as many people as he could in the church, but Jon would probably torch the church anyway, knowing it was Thomas's home. He'd seen the bitterness in Jon's eyes, the resentment at being abandoned by his little brother.

Jon would make it a point to strike someplace close to home for Thomas, to hurt him specifically. He wouldn't kill him. Thomas didn't think that Jon had lost that part of himself that felt some loyalty to his brother. If he had, Thomas wouldn't have survived their last encounter.

But he didn't have any connection to Thomas's

life here except knowing he was a priest. So, the church was an obvious target. But it was also near the middle of town, so the gang wouldn't simply ride in, doing no damage to the rest of the town or its folk, torch the church, then ride out again.

It had no dramatic style, which was one thing Jonathan prided himself on. Everything he did had an element of show to it. If they rode through town, irons would be hot, and anyone they could get in their sights would be a victim.

And if they went that far, Jon would probably just finish riding through town and killing anyone he could in the process.

And Thomas could do nothing. Maybe he should warn people to flee the town until the marshals could arrive and do some good. Or until the Tsawi found the encampment and took care of the issue for all of them. He only prayed that not too many Tsawi or marshals would lose their lives fighting Jon and his boys.

It would help if he could just figure out where they'd strike next, and how. Warning the sheriff could at least allow any innocents to get out of the way before the attack.

If only he wasn't...

"Reverend!" called a voice that instantly brought a smile to his lips, albeit a small one, under the circumstances.

"Mrs. Riley," he said, turning as he tipped his hat to the charmingly quirky woman. "It's a pleasure to see you today. How is living with Mrs. Pomeroy?"

"Oh, lovely," she replied with a smile. "We just sit about and flap our jaws while we knit. We've gotten so much done!"

"Your optimism in the face of adversity is a true inspiration, Mrs. Riley," he told her, only half teasing.

She truly was remarkable. She'd just lost the home she'd built decades ago with her since-deceased husband, along with everything inside it. It hadn't taken long for the house to burn, he remembered. The bucket brigade couldn't do much except keep the flames from spreading to her fields.

"Don't go putting me up on a pedestal, reverend. I'm afraid of heights." She laughed lightly at her jest, and Thomas laughed along with her.

Thomas would build her a new house once this was all resolved, with his own two hands. It wouldn't be the same, but it would be something.

If he survived this. If any of them did.

His laughter faded a little awkwardly, and her keen eyes and ears didn't miss the significance.

Widow Riley eyed him critically, sizing him up, then nodded, deciding something that clearly involved him.

"Come along, reverend," she said, taking his arm and steering him along. He laughed again.

"And where, pray tell, are we heading, Mrs. Riley?"

"To Mrs. Pomeroy's. I'm going to make you

some tea and share an apple cookie or five with you."

"Mrs. Riley, you really don't have to…" he began, but she rolled right over him.

"Oh, tosh. I baked too many, and you look like you need to get a little weight off your chest and add a little to your belly. I can help with both."

He actually pulled against her arm at that and stopped. Thomas had no intention of telling this kind and generous woman anything about what was going on. The sheriff and Rue had both been accepting of his secrets, but he seriously doubted anyone else in town would be.

"Mrs. Riley, I…" Her grip was like iron, and he blinked in surprise at her impressive resistance.

"I don't want to hear it. You can spare half an hour to talk to a lonely old woman. Mrs. Pomeroy is down shopping for a new hat, and good lord, but that woman can shop! She'll be there all day, and I'm all finished with my errands. I'm all tuckered out and want to just go sit, drink some tea, and enjoy the company of a handsome young man. Is that too much to ask?"

Thomas hesitated, unsure of whether to laugh or run.

"Well?" she demanded more sternly. "Is it?"

"No ma'am, I don't believe it is," he conceded, allowing her to pull him along again.

"Good. I don't have to pull you by the ear, then. And don't you think I wouldn't!"

"I have no doubt, Mrs. Riley," he chuckled. "And I admit, apple cookies and tea does sound rather nice. I can't stay long, though. I've got things I need to do today."

"Yes, sir, I could see that from the way you been wandering around town for the last fifteen minutes with no more aim than old Mr. Humphreys after a night at the saloon," she said innocently.

Thomas winced. He hadn't realized he'd been so transparent. He did have things to do... he just didn't know what those things were. Thomas had ideas and options, but none of them were great. None of them guaranteed the safety of the good folk here in Granada.

"Decisions to make first," he replied simply.

This seemed to satisfy the widow, and she nodded, leading him down the road. It wasn't far to the house.

She ushered him inside, sitting him in an upholstered armchair that might possibly have been older than she was. The lacey doily draped over the back of the pale blue armchair had picked up more than a touch of yellow from its own age.

It was all immaculately clean, however, just as Mrs. Pomeroy herself always was, just... old. There was something oddly comforting about it, like he imagined his own grandmother's front room might have looked, had he ever met her. Either one of them, for that matter.

The chair held the faint scent of perfume, but

it wasn't unpleasant. It smelled like a rosebush in the autumn.

"Now, you just sit right there, reverend, and I'll put the kettle on," she said and shuffled into the kitchen.

Thomas leaned back in the old, but surprisingly comfortable chair, and tried to relax. His thoughts wouldn't allow it, as he had known they wouldn't. But something about the comfort and security of the old woman's living room steered his mind away from the trouble with his brother and back to Rue.

Everything seemed to bring his mind back to Rue.

Her level of understanding and patience was incredible. Not to mention her strength and integrity. She'd taken his admissions in full stride, had been forthright and honest about overhearing about his brother, and had given up her whole life to help her sister raise six children. She'd come from a place of hopelessness, not just darkness, but when her sister called, she hadn't hesitated.

But she wasn't afraid to throw a barb or two, and he suspected wasn't afraid to fight when pushed, either. There was a challenging light to her eyes whenever she felt the least threatened or put on the spot that he loved to see. She had fire and spirit but tempered it with experience and introspection. She seemed to understand herself, and as such, understood others better than many.

Rue would make a marvelous mother, he

thought, embarrassing himself at the idea. She'd be a good second mother to those six kids, that was for sure, he corrected himself.

But Rue deserved more than just that. She deserved a husband of her own, children of her own. Not at the expense of her sister, of course, but it wasn't at all uncommon for a widow and her young children to live with her sibling and their spouse and children.

The West wasn't an easy place to live, and widows and widowers weren't all that uncommon. The right man would take that on for Rue.

He would take that on for Rue. But he wasn't the right man, he knew. She also deserved a man she could actually be with, and that man wasn't him.

Widow Riley shuffled back in with a tray piled high with a tea kettle, teacups, a small dish of sugar, a bowl of cream, and a plate overflowing with apple cookies that smelled so good his mouth instantly watered.

"Sorry for the wait, reverend. You're a patient man," she said.

"Patience is a virtue," he replied.

"Certainly is. One that I myself am not blessed with an abundance of, so I sure appreciate it when I see it in others."

"It's my pleasure, Mrs. Riley. It's a very comfortable living room, I didn't mind the wait at all."

"Kind of you. Here, let me pour you a cup. Do

you take cream and sugar?"

"No, ma'am. The tea itself is fine."

"See, you're just like my Ben. He always said he preferred coffee and liked it straight and strong. When I could convince him to have a cup of tea with me, it was always with no cream or sugar. He always said he got enough sugar from me, didn't need it in his food." Widow Riley laughed and shook her head as she poured. "Can you imagine?"

Thomas smiled fondly. He'd never met Ben Riley, but word among the townsfolk was that he was as upstanding a man as they came. He'd help you build a barn or give you the coat from his own back if you needed it. He'd also give you a good punch in the nose, if you needed that instead. Thomas could respect a man like that.

"Sounds like a real card, Mrs. Riley," Thomas said affectionately.

"Oh, he was that, among other things," she chuckled, handing him the cup with one hand, and a pair of soft apple cookies with the other.

"Thank you kindly, Mrs. Riley," he said, accepting both. "Unlike your husband, though, I don't mind the sugar, just don't care for it in my drinks. Your cookies, on the other hand," he said with a wink, holding up one cookie before taking a bite.

The tartness of the apples she'd used beautifully complimented the rich brown sugar that had gone into the baking, accented by a healthy splash of cinnamon. If ever home had a taste, he thought, these cookies would be it. He closed his eyes a moment and reveled in them. Mrs. Riley laughed.

"Oh, come on, now," she said.

"Can't help it, ma'am. When I pass on from this earth, if heaven doesn't have cookies like this, I'm leaving," Thomas replied with a grin. She laughed again.

"If they ain't got them when I get there, you can bet the farm they sure as shoot will after! I'll get there first, so you just be sure and come find me when you get to the other side, and I'll whip you up a fresh batch."

"Now that's an offer I can't refuse, Mrs. Riley," Thomas grinned, taking another bite of the wonderful cookie.

"All right, enough chatter about my cookies. Take yourself a sip of tea, then tell me what's on your mind," she urged.

He took a slow sip of the tea, a subtle but dark brew that played well with the cookies. His sip was slow not to savor, though, but to think.

"Not really sure I can share, Mrs. Riley," he told her reluctantly. "This trouble hereabouts has got my mind in a real storm. Just trying to figure out how to help the best I can."

"Oh, reverend, you help in so many ways! Just your presence calms a lot of folk around this town. You knowing and being friends with the Indians doesn't hurt, though I'd love to hear someday how that little friendship came about."

Thomas almost choked on a cookie. She continued, though, sparing him from feeling obliged to come up with an answer.

"But really, reverend, it's the little things you do. You don't just preach in Sundays, though that's certainly enjoyable enough. You pitch in, you see?"

"Not sure I do, ma'am," he replied.

"You're not afraid to roll up those black sleeves and work up a sweat helping old ladies rebuild cellars, or erecting barns, or digging up stumps in the field. I've seen you offer a ride to people with broken wagon wheels or lame horses, help birth a struggling calf, and bring food to a grieving family while you help them keep up on their chores as they find a new normal."

Thomas swallowed hard, annoyed by the lump forming in his throat. None of what she was saying was wrong, but he didn't do it to be recognized or seen as anything other than doing his job.

"What you bring to the people of this town is more than just the Bible, reverend. You bring them God, and that ain't always the same thing."

"I wish it were, ma'am, but you're right. I just wish, in times like these, that I could do more. Help stand against the wave of darkness, you know?"

"Reverend, can I be candid?"

"Are you ever anything less?" Thomas replied with a chuckle.

"I'm too old to beat around the bush, reverend," she grinned, then grew serious again. "See, what I've seen in you these past few days has me, and a few other folks around here, worried. You've got the look of a man locked in a cage. There's something eating away at you, maybe more than one thing, and you're feeling mighty helpless to do anything about it. Am I right?"

"Pipped the ace, Mrs. Riley," he admitted.

He might not have to tell her anything, he thought in a mixture of awe and trepidation. She might just pluck his worries and secrets straight out of his own mind. Thomas wondered if she had already deduced his relationship to the attackers.

"All you need to do is figure out where your priorities lie. Nothing in this life comes without sacrificing something else to get it. Sometimes it's time, sometimes money, sometimes relationships, sometimes a little blood. But everything costs you something.

"The trick is first to figure out what you really, truly want. Then, figure out what you'd have to give up getting it. Finally, decide if what you'd lose is worth the gain. Sometimes it is, sometimes it ain't. Nobody can tell you that but you, reverend."

"That all makes a lot of sense, Mrs. Riley," he said, chewing on both her words and another cookie.

"So, what would you lose if you pursued that lovely Miss Briggs?" she asked bluntly.

Thomas froze in mid-chew, stunned by the bold question. He considered for a long moment. There was a lot that he could lose in the next few days, and he wasn't even sure where to start. But regarding Rue specifically...

"There isn't anything to lose, Mrs. Riley. My order forbids marriage among the clergy. It isn't a problem, since she and I couldn't be together even if she wanted to."

He almost told her that he didn't love Rue, so why was she even asking, but was suddenly unsure why he couldn't actually say the words.

"That's a big pile o' pig pucky, reverend, if you'll forgive my language. What you're really saying there is that you'd lose your position here. That's what you're afraid of losing if you put your cap in for her."

"Mrs. Riley," he said, but had no argument for her.

That is what he'd be giving up, but he hadn't even really thought about it in terms of walking away from the church as a possibility. It wasn't a possibility. Was it? It was more than his position he'd lose. He'd lose not only his place in the church, but his place in the community along with it.

"Mrs. Riley," he tried again, "there isn't even a question of my giving up the cloth. I made a vow to serve God. Rue and I are not a possibility. She might not even..."

"Oh, she does, reverend," Widow Riley

cackled. "She sure does!"

The certainty with which she said that made his heart leap, then sink hard once again as he considered the implications. Rue couldn't seriously be considering wanting him to leave the church for her.

Something about her asking him to do that bothered him, even if he suddenly couldn't let go of the idea of living with her, raising a family with her…

"She wouldn't ask that of me," he replied, more to reassure himself than anything else.

"You're right, she wouldn't," came the immediate reply. "She's a fine woman, reverend. She won't ask you to give up anything. It's your decision, free and clear, whether you choose to do anything or not. But you two have got a real spark. I've only seen it a handful of times in my life, at least the way you two have it."

"What does that mean?" Thomas asked.

"It means you're making a decision, even if that decision is not to make one. You either give up the cloth and pursue Miss Briggs, or you give up Miss Briggs and hold on to the cloth. Seems pretty simple."

"I made a vow to serve God," he repeated, and it wasn't an idle argument.

That vow to serve God was at the core of the man he'd worked hard to build himself into. If he were to give that up, he might as well give up everything right now and go lie down in a grave.

"There's plenty of ways to do that, reverend. Ways that don't require preaching in church, if you know what I mean. Reverend, do you consider me a godly person?"

"Yes, ma'am," he replied, a little taken aback by her turn. "You're a fine, devout Christian."

"Do you think I serve God?"

Ah, there it was, he realized. Slowly, he responded.

"Yes, ma'am. You bring kindness and laughter all around you. Your soul is a light in this town, and a purer one, I can't imagine."

"Flatterer," she said, patting his hand. "Remember what I told you before?" she asked, more seriously. "You bring God to this town in ways that reach a lot further, and stick in the mind a lot better than a sermon. Don't get me wrong, your sermons are beautiful, and are always uplifting. But when a person is struggling to get by, it isn't often a sermon that truly brings God back to their hearts and minds.

"It's the willing hands bringing them a warm meal, the kind and reassuring word as you help them with a sick child. It's the simple act of serving your fellows with kindness and compassion. That, reverend, is something truly divine. And you do that every day, church or no church."

He leaned back and thought about that. She wasn't wrong. Serving his fellow man was serving

God. He loved his calling. He truly did. But his calling wasn't his service, it was simply the means for his service. It certainly raised some unexpected possibilities.

"So, what about the other problem?" Mrs. Riley interrupted after a long pause.

"The other problem?" he asked, thrown off once more by her quick turns of conversation.

"Miss Briggs is a trouble you've been chewing on, no doubt, but that ain't all that's got you riled."

"I really can't talk about that trouble, Mrs. Riley."

"I understand that, reverend. But the same thought applies. What do you want? What will it cost you? And is it worth it?"

What would it cost him, he considered.

Maybe everything.

But he could lose everything either way.

Damned if he did, and if he didn't.

Chapter Twenty

He knew he wasn't worthy of her. The darkness of his past was too much to inflict on any woman. It wasn't as simple as giving up his position in the church and they'd live happily ever after.

The situation with his brother was more than enough to prove that to him. He couldn't hide from his past. Sooner or later, sheriff or former associate, someone would find him and either arrest him or kill him. Maybe both. In that order, of course.

No. He couldn't pursue Rue.

His initial decision was the right one. She'd find a better man than he ever could be. She deserved a better man than he could ever be.

He would remain in his calling, in his post at the church, helping this town in as many ways as he possibly could. Until the day his past rode in and shot him. Which might be today, come to think of it. He didn't believe Jonathan would shoot him, but he might not tell his men not to.

And Thomas would be nothing more than another helpless target. So be it.

He was heading back to the church after a lovely visit with Widow Riley when a commotion down a side street drew his attention. He heard galloping horses, yells, and whoops.

It had started already.

Turning, he ran as fast as his long legs could carry him toward the commotion. He didn't know what he could possibly do, but he ran anyway.

He was almost upon the ruckus when he realized two things. First, he hadn't yet heard gunshots. Second, he could hear that some of the yelling was in Caddo, the language of the Tsawi.

Rounding the corner, he saw a trio of Tsawi warriors, headed by Red Feather. They were surrounded by townsfolk, a dozen guns aimed at the Tsawi.

The sheriff was there, frantically urging people not to shoot. The two braves beside Red Feather had arrows nocked and drawn, but Red Feather was urging them not to shoot, either.

Not what he'd expected at all.

Calling out in English, he said "Please, put your guns down! These are my friends!"

Switching to Caddo, he said to the warriors, "Stand easy, friends! These people are not your enemy!"

The townsfolk listened first. Not surprising, as the two braves with Red Feather did not know Thomas. But his speech in their tongue caused them to hesitate just long enough for the townsfolk to lower their guns, albeit reluctantly.

The combination of the townsfolk standing down, Thomas calling to them in their own language, and Red Feather telling them Thomas was a friend was enough, and they eased their bows and lowered the arrows.

Neither the townsfolk nor the Tsawi looked comfortable, but nobody was aiming a weapon at anyone. An uneasy truce it may be, but Thomas would gladly take it, and thank God for the gift.

"Red Feather," Thomas said in Caddo, "it is good to see you, but why are you here in town?"

"We come to speak to you," Red Feather replied, breath heavy and words rushed.

"What news?" Thomas asked, knowing they wouldn't have dared enter the town like this if it wasn't urgent.

"We have found your white raiders. They camp today by the northern spring."

"That's excellent news!"

"News is mixed," Red Feather replied. "We have found them, but they arm for war. Three of my scouts have raced back to tell Singing Owl, and we came to tell you. I do not know if either will be in time. They will move quickly."

Thomas digested the news for a few heartbeats, then spoke to the townspeople.

"Get home. Take your families and find someplace to hide. The band of mercenaries that's been attacking the outlying farms is going to be riding through town soon, and they don't plan kindness on anyone they cross. Get yourselves armed but stay cautious. Fight to defend yourself, but we'll all be better off if they come into town and can't find anyone, if it comes to that. The Tsawi ride to help us."

The people frantically took off in all directions at his words. Thomas didn't feel it necessary to translate to the townsfolk that the Tsawi might not arrive in time. He turned to the sheriff.

"Any word on the U.S. Marshals?" he asked. The sheriff shook his head. Thomas nodded.

"All right. You get home to the missus, too, sir. Your gun might take a few of them down, but not enough to matter. Our safest bet is to hide and hope to delay long enough for the Tsawi to reach us."

The sheriff walked up and held out his hand. Thomas shook it.

"Thank you, reverend. Whatever happens, it's an honor to know you."

"You too, sheriff," Thomas said sincerely.

The sheriff then turned and held a hand out to Red Feather, to the surprise of the three braves.

"Reverend, kindly tell these gentlemen that we sincerely appreciate their warning. They've saved a lot of my people's lives today, and I don't intend to forget it."

Thomas translated, and Red Feather smiled, reaching down to shake the sheriff's hand.

With a nod from each, the sheriff turned and

hurried down the road. Thomas glanced around. It was amazing how still and quiet things had gotten, and so quickly.

"Thank you, Red Feather," Thomas said to his friend. "Head out and see if you can't urge a bit more speed from the warriors' horses. A lot of people will probably die today, but your warriors can save a lot of innocent women and children."

"And you?" Red Feather asked. "Will you fight with our warriors?"

Thomas hesitated, then reached up and touched his collar.

"I'm sorry, Red Feather. I can't."

Red Feather looked disappointed but nodded. They turned to leave, but Red Feather stopped, looking back.

"These white raiders," he said. Thomas nodded for him to continue. "They have prisoners."

"What?" Thomas asked, feeling his heart sink into his boots. His bones filled with the chill of dread.

"I do not know how many, or who. White people. At least one woman and two children."

The cold in his bones was abruptly superseded by a sickening lurch in his stomach. His hands shook, and he clenched them to still the trembling.

"Go, Red Feather. As fast as you can," Thomas said in a voice barely above a whisper.

Red Feather nodded, and he and the braves took off at a full gallop back out of town toward the east.

Thomas turned and ran toward the church. His long strides ate up the ground, and it took him less than two minutes to reach the church.

He burst through the rectory doors, calling out.

"Rue! Josie!"

There was no answer.

He raced through the rectory. It was empty. Thomas quickly ran into the chapel, praying with all his heart that they had taken refuge there. He was half right.

Josie sat in one of the pews, praying with several of the children. Marshall and Robbie weren't there.

Neither was Rue.

"Josie!" he called. She looked up and gasped a relieved sob.

"Reverend! Marshall and Robbie snuck off! They took the rifles. I think they went to find the bandits. They'd been talking all morning about protecting us."

"Dear God," Thomas said, voice barely audible. "And Rue?"

"She went after them to try and bring them back as soon as we learned they were gone. I wasn't worried overly much about it, until I heard the news the sheriff brought by. Reverend, please tell me I'll get my boys and my sister back!" She forced words out around her sobs, but Thomas understood her perfectly.

"God willing," he said, for the first time hating the feel of the words in his mouth. His sense of helplessness was overwhelming. "Take the kids and get down into the root cellar under the shed. There's food and water down there, and the entrance isn't plainly obvious. You'll be safe."

"What are you going to do?" Josie asked, rounding up the four younger kids. Lucy and Georgia were sobbing, too.

He truly didn't know.

"Whatever I can, Josie," he replied softly. She nodded and hurried out of the church.

Thomas stood frozen for a long moment, then walked toward the altar. He paused and genuflected, whispering a prayer. His whispered prayer lasted for a long time.

He was useless, he knew. God already knew what was going on and had already laid out the conclusion. His prayer was more because it was all he could do than anything else.

His faith was strong and firm, even this didn't shake it. But his conviction that he was making the right decisions was being battered like a barn door in a tornado.

His order vowed pacifism. God would do as He would. As a man of action, Thomas knew that God often guided men and women to be His instruments, however, and sometimes those instruments were weapons. God's warriors in the Bible were many.

Thou shalt not kill, he reminded himself. But God himself had ordered many battles, wars, and sacrifices that took lives. It was a sticking point he'd never picked at before.

He understood that context mattered, but he didn't know where that line in the sand was. If there was a line.

And if there was a line, surely fighting to protect the innocent from the destruction and horror wrought by wickedness was on the virtuous side of that line.

What would he do, anyway? Go and try to fight the whole gang himself? It was foolish to even consider it, even for him. Until the Tsawi arrived, nobody could make an impact on Jon's plans. The U.S. Marshals might. Might, and only if they brought dozens of men, which they probably wouldn't, and only if they got here in time, which they certainly wouldn't.

But maybe he could stall, he thought. If he could delay Jon's ride on the town by even ten minutes, it might be enough for the Tsawi to catch up. That was something he could do. He would almost certainly not survive the encounter, but maybe he could offer himself as a trade for Rue and the boys, as he was certain now that's who Jonathan had in his camp.

If they were even still alive.

Stop, Thomas almost screamed at himself. Of course they're still alive! Jonathan has them for a reason. Probably leverage against Thomas. If half the town knew about Rue and Thomas, it wasn't out of the question that Jonathan did, too. He almost certainly had scouts of his own watching the town.

That was it, he knew. He had to go meet Jonathan and his men, and try to negotiate for the release of Marshall, Robbie, and Rue. And maybe hold them long enough. It didn't have to be forever, just long enough.

God would decide the rest.

Thomas turned and walked to the votives near one side of the church to light a candle. As he stepped in front of the rack of candles, a floorboard creaked. He frowned. There were a few creaky boards in this church, but that wasn't one of them. He'd stood here a thousand times since coming to Granada, and the board had never creaked before.

In a flash, he understood. The board didn't usually creak because he'd sealed it down tightly a few years before. He knew what was under that board. He'd all but forgotten.

He knelt slowly, almost reverently. His heart pounded in his chest with an intensity that made his ears ring. Filled with fear, trepidation, and reverence, he drew a penknife and began working at the board.

It had creaked loudly.

It never creaked. Why now?

He suspected he knew the answer to that question.

Pulling up the board at last, his eyes fell on the oilcloth-wrapped package within. Drawing it out, he was surprised to see his fingers were rock steady as he moved to untie the twine binding. His fingers paused on the thin cord, feeling the rough texture of the twine beneath his fingertips.

This was it, he knew. This was the moment where he wouldn't be able to turn back. His next movement would be his final decision. He could put the package back, replace the board, and light a candle.

Or, he could untie the knot and cast off his calling forever. Not for love, not for honor, but to slay a demon.

If the Tsawi rode up while Thomas was talking to Jonathan, Jonathan would immediately kill the hostages. Thomas knew that without the slightest doubt. His willingness to release them for Thomas was a slim hope, as well. While Jonathan breathed, death crowded around him like vultures to a carcass.

He reveled in it. Thrived on pain and torment. While he lived, others would die. Rue, Marshall, and Robbie likely first today, probably followed by Thomas himself, but then more people. A lot more.

Before he realized what he was doing, his hands had made the decision for him. The knot came untied in his traitorous fingers, and the oilcloth fell away from the contents.

The achingly familiar glint of well-polished black and gold metal, and the smell of the darkly oiled leather holsters shattered any doubts.

He'd been lying to himself. His whole adult life, he'd been lying to himself. He wasn't a monster. Not truly. His actions in years gone spoke otherwise, but he'd never embraced suffering the way Jonathan had. Thomas had found his way out of the darkness and learned to live a wholesome, compassionate life.

But he also wasn't a priest. Not truly.

In title and position, certainly, but not in his heart. He was and always would be a fighter. For all the wrong reasons initially, and in all the wrong ways. Then for slightly better reasons, but then no longer.

Today, he would fight once more. Against the evil that had consumed his brother. Against the destruction of hundreds of innocent men, women, and children, here and in the future at the hands of the monster that was Jonathan Jarrett.

Against the loss of the woman he loved.

And he did love her, he knew in that instant. He had loved her since the day they'd met, not that long ago. Her soul spoke to his beyond words or time.

With a conviction he'd been lacking for longer than he could remember, he stood smoothly and buckled the gun belt around his waist with an ease that spoke of years of familiarity. For a moment, he rested his hands on the black and gold guns now at his hips. There was a reassurance there, a comforting familiarity.

With this action, he knew his life as a priest, as a well-considered member of this beautiful community, was over. It had been over the day Jon Jarrett rode to Granada. This could only have ended with the death of one or the other of the Jarrett brothers.

There was no time to waste, he reminded himself, snapping out of his mental realignment with a new focus.

Rue and the boys were in danger. The entire town was in danger. The Tsawi were coming, but he knew they wouldn't be in time. The U.S. Marshals were coming, but they wouldn't be in time, either.

Thomas had to stall them.

Just long enough.

He reached a hand up and pulled the white tab from his collar, regarding it for a moment before dropping it.

He was halfway out the door before it touched the ground.

Chapter Twenty-One

Rue snarled at the man leering at her. Or rather, the best she could snarl around the dirty cloth bound around her head and between her teeth. He laughed riotously, reaching a hand out to grope her. Marshall tried to push between them, but he didn't need to.

"Hey!" shouted a sharp, angry, menacing voice. The man pulled back and looked at his boss, who stalked over. "She's not for you. Not for any of you. She's for my brother. If you put so much as one greasy finger on her, I'll kill you."

"Yes, boss. Sorry, boss," said the man, backing away, but scowling darkly at Rue. She returned it in spades.

Marshall, who had so nobly tried to intervene the best he could in his own bound state, leaned over and rested a head on her shoulder. She leaned her head on his, too. Robbie, never one to be left out, scooted over and leaned into his brother.

She wished she could tell them it would all be all right. But she didn't know whether it would or not. Even if she could speak, which she couldn't at the moment.

The only comfort she had was that the leader, Thomas's brother Jon, she remembered with a sinking feeling in her gut, wouldn't let the men rape her. That would have been bad enough, but in front of the boys?

She shivered a little at the thought despite sitting so near the warm spring where she'd once shared a moment with Thomas. She and the boys sat along the rocks beside the water, its steam warming her hands bound behind her back.

But why was she to be untouched, she wondered. Jonathan had said she was for Thomas. What did he mean by that?

The men all around her, a darker, dirtier, more vicious-looking group of men than she'd ever seen in her life, and she'd seen some pretty sketchy gents, were arming themselves for battle. The number of pistols, rifles, and shotguns catching and throwing back the dappled sunlight was impressive, in a terrifying, heart-stopping kind of way.

The men were preparing to ride out, and she and the boys were hauled to their feet and guided toward the horses.

Thomas, she said in her mind, please find someplace to hide. They're going to kill you.

A sharp whistle caused all the men to pause in their various activities. She looked over at Jonathan. He grinned.

"Saved us a trip, boys! My brother has come to us!" he said with a laugh. Her heart sank and her eyes closed, tears pushing toward the surface.

The men laughed, too, but Rue notice an odd hesitance and anxiety in the men at the words. They were casting nervous glances down toward the trail. It took her a moment to realize something astonishing. These men were afraid of Thomas. The whole group of these brutish ruffians feared him.

Rue truly wouldn't have guessed that anyone could scare men like this, but the evidence was right before her. The man who'd tried to grope her kept touching his gun belt, as if to reassure himself it was there, and mopping sweat from his brow with a dirty handkerchief, despite the weather being fairly cool.

She knew Thomas had been a member of this gang once, but it was obvious now that he'd been more than that. Thomas Jarrett was a name known, and feared, in this circle.

The men pulled back and formed a crowd behind and to the sides of Jonathan, leaving the south open. Rue and the boys were pulled into position to Jonathan's side. One man held each of them, each man drawing a gun and holding it to their temples. She tried to stop her trembling, trying to comfort the boys with her calmness.

She could hear Robbie crying quietly into his gag.

But all they could do was wait and see.

It didn't take long.

Thomas walked slowly out of the tree line, steadily and gracefully moving toward his brother.

Her breath caught in her throat.

The man she saw now wasn't a priest. The mask had melted away from him to reveal the man beneath. The white collar was gone, and a pair of strikingly beautiful guns hung at his hips, but it was more than that. It was in his face, his posture, but most especially his eyes.

Oh, Thomas, she thought to herself, what have you done?

The man she saw walking toward them now was the man she'd seen in the church before he'd gone to tell the sheriff about his brother. Only magnified.

His presence was palpable, power and predatory confidence radiating from him like the steam from the spring behind them. Thomas appeared calm but was focused with an intensity unlike any she'd ever seen.

His hawk eyes were locked on his brother's, and an air of death seemed to radiate from him. This man was a killer.

But for one brief instant, his eyes flicked to her. Her heart surged at the glimmer of warmth she saw in his icy eyes as he did so.

Jonathan saw it, too. She saw his smile grow smugly as she glanced at the mercenary leader.

"Tommy, so glad you could make it," Jonathan said as Thomas stopped ten feet from them.

"Let them go, Jon," Thomas said. His voice held the same steel his eyes did, and Rue felt her skin chill at the menace in it.

"I actually thought we might just start our day's bloodbath with them. I saved them for you, though. You want to kill them, or just watch while we do?"

"I won't tell you again, Jon. Let them go."

"So arrogant!" Jonathan laughed. "Look at you. Strutting up here like you own the place, ignoring the two dozen guns aimed at you right now, and giving me orders. Me! Even you can't get out of this one alive, little brother."

"I ain't aiming to," Thomas replied.

This gave Jonathan pause. Rue watched as the man's smug smile slipped a little.

"Have you lost your mind? I mean, I knew the whole priest thing was a sham, but I didn't know you were looking to meet your maker for real."

"I'm offering you a deal, Jonny," Thomas said.

Jonathan considered a moment, uncertainty flickering in his eyes.

"What could you possibly offer me?" Jonathan said at length. "I'm about to do what I came here to do, over your dead body if I have to, do a bit of looting, and then go collect the biggest payday we've ever seen. You're a broken-down gunfighter living in a pit in Kansas and pretending to be a priest in a two-pony town. What have you got that I would want?"

"Me," Thomas replied.

"I could kill you right now," Jonathan said dismissively, holding his arms out grandly, indicating his men, who were indeed holding dozens of guns aimed at Thomas. "I don't need to give you anything in return for that."

"You think you're better than me," Thomas said coolly. "You've always thought you were better than me. I'm offering you a chance to prove it."

"What do you mean?" Jonathan asked, frowning. Rue suspected he knew exactly what Thomas meant, however, as his eyes glittered eagerly.

"Just you and me. From right where we stand. If you let those three go first, we'll do it proper. If you don't, you'll have to gun me down in cold blood. Not very satisfying, I'd think. Wasted opportunity." Thomas said.

His lack of emotion as he discussed his own death was chilling. Rue was shivering, though from the comment or the fear of him dying, she wasn't sure.

Maybe both.

"Then what?" Jonathan asked. "Just for the sake of argument, say you win. Which you won't. But let's just say you did. Then what? You kill as many of my men as you can, but there will still be more than enough of them left to kill your girlfriend and the two pups here. Then they ride through town, burning and killing, maybe having a little fun with some of the womenfolk and girls along the way, and you've gained nothing. You have twelve bullets, Tommy. You can't kill us all."

"I don't mean to kill all of you," Thomas said.

Very slowly, Thomas reached a hand down to his left gun. She could feel as much as hear the collective intake of breath and nervous lean backward from the crowd. Jonathan held a hand up to stop anyone from firing just yet. He eyed Thomas curiously, but warily.

Thomas drew the gun slowly, carefully, tripped the release, and dumped all six bullets from the gun onto the dirt, dropping the gun alongside them.

Slowly, he drew his other gun and tripped the release. He slowly drew out one bullet from the chamber, dumped the remaining five rounds in the dirt, and put the one bullet back in, slowly holstering the gun once more. His eyes never left Jonathan's.

"Just you," Thomas finished with an eerie steadiness.

Jonathan stared, astonished. His face was a picture of warring emotions, struggling between worry, uncertainty, overconfidence, and a dose of amusement.

Finally, he laughed.

"Little brother, you've gone crazier than a rabid possum. But I'm going to tell you how this is going to go. We draw down. I kill you. I then kill the pretty lady and the pups, and slaughter everyone in Granada. I get paid. The end."

"And if I win?" Thomas asked. Jonathan

laughed again.

"If you win, which you won't, my men will gun you down, then kill the pretty lady and the pups, and slaughter everyone in Granada. Then they get paid. Either way, you, the lady, the brats, and the town give up the ghost, and my men get paid."

Thomas didn't flinch. He was steady, cold, and calm as a rock in the storm.

But she noticed the man beside Jonathan, his second, she thought, was looking nervously back and forth between them brothers.

Thomas slowly shook his head.

"Here's the offer. You let those three go, and we draw down. You win, I can't do anything to stop anything else you've got planned. But I want you to order your men, right now, that if I win, they ride out of Granada and never come back."

"Quite the stakes there, little brother."

"You know me. I never do anything halfway."

"No, sir, you sure don't," Jonathan laughed. "All right, little brother. I agree. Men, if this boy here puts a bullet in me, you all just ride on out of here. Go get a new contract somewhere else. McCabe here will lead the gang."

The man to his side smiled smugly and drew himself up proudly. It was actually rather pathetic, Rue thought.

"Happy?" Jonathan asked.

"They go free first, or no deal," Thomas replied.

Jonathan sighed and shook his head.

"Fine, but we're still going to kill them after I put a slug between your eyes," Jonathan said.

He gestured, and Rue felt a knife slide between her bound wrists, a nerve-wracking moment of cold and tension, and then her hands were free. She quickly removed her gag and helped the boys free.

She leaned down close to them and whispered "Run home, boys. Find your mama and look after her and the little ones."

"What about you?" Robbie asked, tears on his cheeks and in his voice.

"I'll be all right, but you need to get. They need looking after. Now! Go!" she replied sharply.

Robbie hesitated, but Marshall gave her a surprisingly knowing, mature look, grabbed his little brother, and hauled him away as fast as their legs could carry them.

Jonathan and Thomas both watched her as she stood upright again, and then didn't move.

Thomas's expression showed his growing concern. Jonathan's showed a growing smile.

"Would you look at that, boys? She wants to watch her man die!" Jonathan said.

She could hear the nervousness in his voice, though. So could his men. None of them laughed.

Rue's eyes turned in fear to Thomas. He was focused on his brother as if they were the only two people in the entire world. She focused on Thomas in much the same way.

"All right, little brother. You ready?" Jonathan asked. Thomas gave a single nod. "All right, on the count of three. One, tw-"

Without warning, Jonathan reached for his gun early. Rue saw it out of the corner of her eye. Her scream of warning died in her throat at the sound of the gunshot.

For a long moment, she couldn't quite process what had happened.

She hadn't blinked. She was sure of it. But she hadn't seen Thomas move. One moment, he stood still as the stones beneath his feet, hands at his sides. The next, his gun was in his hand, as if by magic. He held it now where it had appeared, right at his hip, barrel level with his waist.

Never in her life had she seen anything move that fast. Not a man, not a snake, not even a bolt of lightning. She hadn't even seen him move.

Her eyes turned with morbid gravity toward Jonathan.

To her surprise, Jonathan's gun was in his hand, but the barrel hadn't even finished cleared the holster yet. His eyes were wide with shock

Her eyes moved to the crowd. The staring eyes all around were filled with awe, wonder, and no small amount of fear.

A full second later, Jonathan fell to the ground without a word. No cry, no gasp of pain, nothing. He just fell.

Looking back to Thomas, she could see the

steeliness in his eyes was gone.

Now, his gray gaze, locked on the body of his brother, was filled with a pain far deeper than a physical one. One step, then another, he moved forward. The crowd of mercenaries all stepped back away from him, avoiding him like he was a plague-bearer. All except McCabe.

Thomas slowly holstered his empty gun.

McCabe stared in horror and fury at the body of his boss. He looked up at the approaching Thomas, quickly drew his gun and leveled it at Thomas's head.

"You killed him!" McCabe shouted.

"Yes," Thomas said simply, but the word was one of deepest resignation, not merely an acknowledgement of fact.

"You don't have any bullets left, cowboy," McCabe snarled, "but even if you did, I'd kill you before you could get a shot off."

"I've spilled all the blood I care to, McCabe. The rest of the blood spilled today won't be on my hands."

"You're right. It'll be on mine. Starting with yours."

"You'd best get on with it," Thomas told him, seemingly unconcerned about the gun pointed between his eyes. "The Tsawi know where we are. And they're not happy about you lot killing their scouts and trying to frame them for all the damage you've done here. They're riding here at a gallop, a hundred warriors strong."

McCabe's eyes widened in sudden panic.

"You're lying, preacher," he snarled, though he clearly wasn't so sure, his finger twitching on the trigger.

Thomas didn't flinch.

"I'm not a preacher anymore," he said softly. The regret in his voice broke Rue's heart. She ached for what he'd given up to confront his brother. But in so doing, he'd saved her life and that of the boys.

Well, the boys, anyway. She was still firmly in the thick of things, she realized uncomfortably.

"And you really don't have long," Thomas continued. "Definitely not long enough to raid the town. Maybe not even long enough to get clear of here. Ride out now, while you can," Thomas urged.

"I have long enough to kill you," McCabe spat.

A single arrow flashed in from the east, piercing perfectly through McCabe's extended wrist. He screamed and dropped the gun from his now limp hand.

"No, you don't," Thomas said calmly.

The whoops of a horde of Tsawi was heard even over the rapidly-building earthquake rumble of their galloping horses.

It was hard to see them through the trees, but glimpses of them were already visible. But, somewhat nearer, three braves sat astride their horses. The one in the lead, a tall man with a brilliant red feather tied into his hair that was so bright she could see it from here, lowered his bow with a self-satisfied smile.

Rue stared in awe. She hadn't thought a bow could range that far. Whoever that man was, she thought, he was a marksman of uncanny skill.

The crowd erupted in sudden panic as the reality of their situation sank past the rapid-fire shocks of the last ten minutes.

Men mounted horses frantically, firing blindly toward the oncoming Tsawi as they turned to race as fast as they could in the opposite direction.

In seconds, Rue stood in what felt like the eye of a storm. A brief stillness before the madness erupted again as the mercenaries rode hard away from them.

Their solitude lasted only a few seconds more, long enough for Thomas to fall to his knees beside the body of his brother. Then, the Tsawi were upon them. Parting around them like the surf on a rock, the horsemen curved around, leaving them a circle twenty feet in diameter with them untouched in the center.

The horses and men seemed to go on for a long time before, suddenly, the last of them was past, the sounds of the horde rapidly dwindling.

Then, they were truly alone.

Just Rue and Thomas.

And the body of Jonathan Jarrett.

Chapter Twenty-Two

Rue looked on helplessly as Thomas knelt, cradling his brother's body. Her heart was torn in a thousand pieces for him, and she knew it cast not the glimmer of a candle on the pain he was feeling.

Cautiously, she knelt beside him. His steely gray eyes turned toward her to reveal their transformation. They no longer looked like polished steel. They were dark, gloomy storm clouds of gray, their rain moistening his eyes.

"Thomas," she said, putting an arm around him. He leaned into her.

"There was no other way," he said, voice hitching. "No other way."

"You saved a lot of lives today," she said softly, hoping futilely to ease his guilt over taking the life of his beloved brother.

"No," he replied. "I didn't. I traded the townsfolk for the mercenaries. The Tsawi won't leave a single one of those men alive."

"Hundreds of innocent lives traded for the lives of a few dozen killers?" she asked. He shook his head.

"All life is sacred, Rue. All of it. Some of those men might have someday come out of the darkness. Like I did. Like Jack did. Like Santiago, Storm-Chaser, Lucky, and Kid Grady did. They'll never have the chance for redemption."

"How many lives would they have taken before then? Not just here in Granada. What about after? How many innocent people have been spared because of your actions today? You're a hero, Thomas."

Again, he shook his head.

"I'm a killer, Rue. I always have been. Always will be. So many lives lost at my hands. So much blood…"

"Would you have preferred someone take your life years ago, before you'd had a chance to reform?" she asked. It wasn't an idle question. She genuinely wanted to know the answer.

His eyes turned back to his brother, cradled in his lap.

"Rue, if I could give my life to bring back even a single innocent life I've taken, I'd stand and do so without hesitation."

"A fair trade?" she asked.

"Unquestionably."

"Then remember that when you consider how many innocents you saved today. It cost you a lot. More than anyone can ever know or understand, but you fought to save lives today. And you succeeded.

I'm alive because of you. Marshall and Robbie are alive because of you. Josie, Georgia, Lucy, Mark, and Thomas are all alive because of you. Annie Waterston and her family. Sheriff Rawlins. Widow Riley. All of them. All of us. Because of you."

Thomas took a deep, shaky breath, and nodded.

"I know. You're right. It was necessary. But the price... Rue, I've lost everything. My calling, my position, my reputation in the community, my brother... everything."

"You still have me," Rue said.

Looking up at her again, his eyes held an intensity different, though no less focused, than what they'd held before.

A warmth spread through her body that transcended thought.

"You'll always have me," she repeated more strongly. "Even if we can't be together because of your priesthood. I won't let you give that up for me. I'll take friendship, though, if it's still offered."

She may not be able to be with him the way she wanted to, but she would spend every moment she could with him in whatever ways he was permitted.

Thomas shook his head slowly as she spoke.

"My priesthood is forfeit after..." she saw his eyes start to move down to his brother's body, but they resisted. "Anyway, that doesn't matter. I'll be run out of town after this. And you've got to care for your sister and the kids. You can't leave them, and I wouldn't let you even if you tried. They need you, Rue."

She took a deep breath, then let it out in a low, resigned sigh. He was probably right. On all counts. An idea struck her.

"Thomas, we can hide this. We can say someone else shot…" she stopped, unable to say it. "We can make sure nobody knows you had anything to do with any of this."

"It won't work, Rue," he replied. "You know, the sheriff knows, Marshall and Robbie aren't stupid. They saw the lead-up. They'll know. Sooner or later, word will get out, and it'll be over for me."

"Will you run?" she asked.

"Would you let me if I did?" he asked. The question had a different weight, now that she knew the full truth of him.

"Yes," she said, again without hesitation. "Perhaps that's best. You could start over someplace else."

"No," he replied. "I'm done with that. Once was hard enough. Besides," he added, "I'm so tired of the secrets and lies. I'm not a bad man, Rue. But I was. God above knows I was. Justice should be served for what I've done, no more or less than it has been for my brother."

"So now what?" she asked. A thousand scenarios pushed through her mind, none of them with pleasant outcomes.

"I go back, let everyone know they're safe. I call

a meeting at the church, and tell the community who, and what, I really am. Then, I let them turn me in to the U.S. Marshals, whenever they finally show up. And justice will be done."

A sound came from behind them. She looked back over Thomas's shoulder and her stomach gave a sickening twist. Many of his options had just disappeared.

"Do you have a plan B?" she asked. He looked back, and she saw the resignation fall across his face.

The sheriff, along with four dozen other men of the town, were approaching. All were heavily armed, wary, and confused as they looked about.

Thomas gently laid his brother to the grass and stood, turning to face the music head-on. She couldn't help but admire his courage. Even if she thought he'd be better off running. The idea that the folk of Granada would be the ones to put the nail in his coffin was too much to bear.

"Sheriff," Thomas said as he approached.

The sheriff, and many of the men, noticed both the gun belt around Thomas's waist, and the conspicuous absence of his collar. Quiet, whispered words were shared between a number of them. The whispers didn't sound surprised, though, which caused a furrow in Rue's brow. Something strange was going on.

Thomas slowly drew his remaining pistol out with two fingers, carefully holding it out to the sheriff.

The sheriff looked at the gun in confusion, then back up to Thomas.

"What in the Sam Hill you giving me that for?" he asked. The sheriff gestured at the revolver in his hand. "I already got one. What happened here, reverend?"

Thomas frowned, looking around at the other men. They had gathered around. The rest of the men couldn't help but have seen his gun, and many would have noticed his white collar tab was missing, too.

"I resigned," Thomas said.

"What?" asked Mr. Burley, the barber. "What would you go and do a fool thing like that for?"

"I'm no priest," he tried to explain. "I mean, I am, but it's not the right calling for me, much as I love this town. Now's as good a time as any to confess to you all," he said, but was cut off by Sam Waterston.

"Don't you go saying anything foolish, Mr. Jarrett," he said. Rue noticed he'd dropped the 'reverend' honorific, but otherwise, his tone was no different than usual. "We just had us a conversation with the two U.S. Marshals the feds sent our way."

"Two?!" Thomas all but exploded. "They sent two men? Didn't you tell them it was Jonathan Jarrett?" he demanded of the sheriff.

"I sure did, but they were more concerned with another rumor they'd heard," Sheriff Rawlins said.

"Rumor?" Thomas asked, tone puzzled.

Rue was puzzled, too. None of this made any sense.

"That's right," Sam Waterston continued. "Someone told the marshals that a killer name of Thomas Jarrett was in hiding out here in town. Seems they were more concerned about this Jarrett than the other one with the gang attacking our town. Government priorities, am I right?" He chuckled.

Rue and Thomas shared a look, and then simply stared at the men.

"Anyway," Sheriff Rawlins took up the story, "they had a wanted poster and everything they showed us. See, we'd heard you were coming up north to try and rescue Miss Briggs and the boys, and we were rallying to come and give you a hand. That's why we're all here now, though looks like you've got things well enough in hand."

"They had a wanted poster?" Rue asked, surprised.

It was another piece of Thomas's puzzle she hadn't considered. Of course there would have been wanted posters, with his life the way it had been those years ago. She'd just never thought about it.

"Sure did. Good artist, too. Lifelike drawing," Mr. Burley added. "They showed it to the lot of us."

"But," Thomas started, but fell back a step, at a loss. Rue put a steadying hand on his arm.

"So, we all give that poster a real good look, see," Mr. Edwards, the farrier said, "and then told those two government boys the truth."

"You did." Thomas said more than asked, still confused.

Rue couldn't blame him. If the townsfolk had been told about his past and showed his picture, then told the U.S. Marshals the truth, why in the world wasn't he under arrest right this moment?

"Sure did," Mr. Burley said, puffing his chest up smugly.

"That's right," Sam Waterston agreed. "We told those two government boys that there were no killers anywhere near this town name of Thomas Jarrett, but if we ever saw a man like that, we'd be sure to let them know."

Thomas's balance shifted, and Rue's steadying hand supported more of his weight. She looked at him sharply. He wasn't fainting, but he was sure stunned. Not that she blamed him, under the circumstances.

"Anyway," Mr. Edwards continued, "we sent those boys on their way. Told them we'd already run off Jonathan Jarrett and his boys, and they were free to go. They didn't waste any time in hitting the hills," he chuckled. "I guess the idea of the forty of us all armed the way we were when they showed up saying we'd just run off the Jarrett Gang and looked not a scratch among us spooked them. They didn't even ask any more question about that Thomas Jarrett fella."

"We figured with just two of them," Sheriff

Rawlins added, "they wouldn't be of much extra help up here when the bullets started flying, and could cause a whole heap of trouble for you, if they got it into their heads to confuse you with the man from that poster. Even though we told them plain you ain't him."

"And we wasn't lying, neither," Mr. Abrams added, speaking for the first time. "That man ain't you. I might just be tossing a spin here, but I'd be wagering the man they're after died years ago."

Thomas looked like he couldn't decide whether to fall to his knees or hug the first person he could reach.

"I'd say you might just be right on that point, Mr. Abrams," Thomas agreed weakly.

"That's what I figured," Mr. Abrams smugly proclaimed with a decisive nod.

Thomas looked at Rue, and in his eyes, she saw something she hadn't seen in them for a long time.

Hope.

These people weren't stupid, Rue knew. Quite the contrary. If they'd heard his name in that context, seen his picture, heard he was wanted by the feds, and then come up here to find him with guns at his waist and a dead man in his arms, they knew full well who Thomas was.

But, she thought, realizing the profundity of that statement, they knew who Thomas was then, but more than that, they knew who he was now. And they, as a community, had rallied unspoken to support their reverend. Their friend.

Tears came unbidden to her own eyes, and Thomas looked quickly away, as if the sight of her tears would be the final push over the edge he teetered on so precariously.

"Anyway," Sheriff Rawlins said, looking around, "we saw the Briggs boys coming down. They're just fine. But without Miss Briggs here with them, we hurried on up as fast as we could. Figured you might need a hand. Figured wrong, looks like."

"The Tsawi arrived in time," Thomas said with a smile.

"I owe those fellas a few cases of whiskey," Sheriff Rawlins said with a nod.

"A lot of cases of whiskey," Thomas corrected with a laugh. "They must have had near on a hundred braves. Ran the whole gang off, though I sincerely doubt any of them will make it even as far as the county border. The Tsawi are a determined folk, and their ponies might be small, but they've got a fair shake more stamina than their quarry will be expecting."

"Can't say I'm sorry to hear that," Sheriff Rawlins said. His eyes finally moved to Jonathan's body. "I am sorry for this, though."

"Me too, sheriff," Thomas said, the regret audible in his voice to anyone with ears. The men around them exchanged sorrowful glances.

The sheriff bent down and checked Jonathan's pulse, but nobody expected anything other than what happened. No pulse was there to find.

Glancing down, the sheriff frowned, reaching for Jonathan's vest pocket. Drawing out the object that had caught his eye, the sheriff began to read the official-looking document he'd discovered.

Rue moved to try and peer over his shoulder, but Thomas was faster and obstructed her view. A few moments passed, then Thomas spoke.

"Governor Delano?" he said thoughtfully to himself, with a note of concern.

The sheriff must have caught the note of recognition in his voice, because he looked up sharply. An unspoken conversation happened between the two men in the span of three heartbeats, then the sheriff nodded, tucking the document into his pocket.

"We'll talk later, Mr. Jarrett," Sheriff Rawlins said firmly. Thomas nodded. The sheriff looked up at the other men. "You boys gather up the body and bring it back to town. Take it straight to Stone's shop, he'll get it ready for a proper funeral."

Nobody asked any questions, like why they were giving a funeral to a man who had just tried to murder their entire town. Everybody understood.

The sheriff clapped Thomas on the shoulder as he passed, and Thomas gave him a grateful nod. Several men gathered up Jonathan's body and began to respectfully convey it back into the trees toward town.

One of the men stopped in front of Thomas

and handed him his fallen gun, and a handful of bullets. He gave Thomas a clap on the shoulder too, before following the rest. Soon, only Rue and Thomas remained.

"Good folk here," she said with a smile. Thomas chuckled and nodded.

"The best."

Rue looked at Thomas, who held an arm out to her with a small smile. The emotions churned like a tornado in his eyes, but he was stronger than the storm, she knew. He'd survive.

And so would she.

Chapter Twenty-Three

"A rail line," Thomas clarified, saying it for the third time in as many minutes. He was struggling to get his mind around it.

"Looks to me like Lieutenant Governor Delano is digging his fingers into the murkier side of his business," Sheriff Rawlins said.

The two sat in the sheriff's office the day after the confrontation, analyzing the document they'd found in Jonathan's pocket.

"Deeper than he already had. Last I knew, he was trying to marry off his daughter to the son of the sheriff," Thomas said. "I'm betting now he was doing it to convince the sheriff to look the other way from anything shady that might come across his desk regarding the lieutenant governor."

"The contract itself isn't incriminating," the sheriff said with evident regret. "There's nothing in it tying him to anything illegal."

"But the fact that Jonathan had it, and that the contract is for control of government-appropriated land running straight through the middle of

Granada for a railroad, and the fact that the land in question is still privately owned by citizens here… I'd bet my last dollar that the lieutenant governor hired Jon and his gang to clear out both us and the Tsawi."

"Think he'd have managed it?" the sheriff asked.

"He had a good plan. Attack the town and the Tsawi, then frame each for the other. Get them to fighting, and the most likely outcome is that the Tsawi would end up wiping out the townsfolk, drawing the wrath of the U.S. Army, which would draw them here in force to wipe out the Tsawi. Government steps in and claims the land, sells via that contract to the unnamed party at the bottom. Lieutenant Governor Delano, along with his unnamed partner, both walk away with a very tidy profit."

"Thank God you were here," Sheriff Rawlins said with a smile.

"Thank God indeed," Thomas chuckled.

A knock came at the door.

"Come on in," Sheriff Rawlins called.

The door opened, and Rue walked in.

Thomas couldn't stop the surge of warmth through his body at the sight of her. She was beautiful, elegant, and smiled at him in a way that drew his eyes unerringly to her lips.

"Gentlemen," she said, "I don't mean to interrupt, but we've cleared out of the rectory, and I was hoping to speak to the rev… to Mr. Jarrett before we rode back to our farm."

Thomas looked to the sheriff, who nodded. He was going to do more research, try to find out who the unnamed party at the bottom of the contract might be. They'd talk later.

Thomas returned the nod and walked out right behind Rue.

He offered his arm and couldn't suppress his pleasure when she took it with another smile.

"Thomas," she started. He loved hearing her say his name. "I wanted to thank you, for everything."

"Nothing, ma'am," he said. She gave him a wry grin at his formality.

"It's wasn't nothing, Thomas, and you know it. We put you out of your own home for days, and then got ourselves into a fix that nearly got you killed."

"None of that was your fault, or the fault of any of your family. The blame lies on Jonathan, pure and simple. He brought all of this down on us. And on himself."

"In any case, I wanted to thank you. You've been nothing but gracious and generous with our family since the day we got here, and it means the world to me, and to Josie."

Thomas was quiet for a long moment, reflecting.

"It's meant a great deal to me, too," he

admitted.

"Are you going to return to the church?" she asked. He just shrugged.

"Yes and no. I'll return and get things tidied and prepared for my replacement. I've already written a letter requesting release from my vows. I aim to send it off tomorrow. I'll keep things running until he gets here."

"And then what?" she asked, stopping him within sight of the church. She turned to face him directly. "You leaving town?"

His mind drifted for a moment to the wonderful people here in Granada. Nowhere else would he find someplace so full of love and forgiveness. Forgiveness grew in this place like wildflowers on the plains. He couldn't even begin to wrap his head around the love he'd received here.

The entire town had to know about his past by now. None seemed too troubled by it. Every man and woman in town seemed to be showing him nothing but support. He got a great deal more grief from his admission that he was giving up his position here as their pastor than from anything else. He'd heard more than a few protests over that one.

But his mind was made up.

He'd been a truly wicked man. And then tried to be a saintly one. It was time he took up ground somewhere in the middle and settled for just being a good one. The best he could be, sure, but being a good man was all he found he really wanted.

A good man with a good life. Maybe with a good wife. He glanced back at Rue, who was watching him closely.

"No," he said firmly, "I won't leave Granada."

The relief in her face was evident, but she hesitated before speaking.

"I'm sorry," she said.

Thomas frowned.

"For what?" he asked, genuinely confused.

"I know that… things between us…" She took a breath and tried again. "Anyway, I know it's been a problem. I never meant to stand between you and your faith," she clarified.

Thomas was touched.

"You never have, Rue," he said softly, gently touching her cheek with the tips of his fingers. "Not once. It's one of many things I love about you. You've always respected both my faith and my calling."

"You love many things about me?" she asked with a coy smile.

Thomas decided this wasn't the time to be playful or beat around the bush. If he didn't say it now, he didn't know when he'd have the courage to say it again.

"I love everything about you, Rue."

Her playful smile slipped at both his words and the emotion in his voice.

"Wh-what?" she asked, clearly stunned by so

direct an admission.

"I love you, Rue," he said again, astonished at the weight he felt flying free from his chest at the words. "I think I have since you first threw a glare at me on that first day in church. And it's all right, it really is, if you don't, you know, feel the same."

"Thomas," she breathed in a way that made his knees weak. But then she inhaled sharply and shook her head. "Thomas, I think you know how I feel about you, but it doesn't change the fact that there's something you don't know about me."

Thomas paused, wracking his brain to figure out what she meant. It took him entirely too long to remember her own darkness, her own past and secrets. He didn't know what hell she'd been through. She knew all his secrets, but he didn't yet know hers.

"Tell me," he said, "so we can give this courtship a real go." He smiled at her in what he hoped was a playful, if comforting way. She smiled briefly, then looked away.

"You don't want me, Thomas."

"You know better than that, Rue," he argued, a knot of concern growing in his chest.

"No good man would," she said. He could hear tears coming into her voice.

"Tell me, Rue." His voice was firm, but gentle. She needed to release the weight of her secrets every bit as much as he had.

"I can't," she said, her voice catching on a

suppressed sob.

"Tell me, Rue," he said even more softly, gently reaching up to touch and lift her chin.

"I'm a ruined woman, Thomas," she finally blurted out.

"What?" he asked, not sure he understood.

"I fell in love once," she began. "I almost ran away with him, but I caught him with another girl. I was crushed. I sobbed for days. Finally, another boy found me crying and came to comfort me. I was upset, and he was so sweet, and we… you know."

"Rue, is that all?" Thomas said, baffled that such a little thing would have caused her so much concern about never being wanted again. It was frowned upon, more so in some towns than others, but not unheard of.

"No!" she snapped, pushing him back a step, tears on her cheeks as she turned hot and angry eyes up at him.

Thomas stared in shock but waited for her to continue. It took her a moment, but she did.

"People found out. My father found out. He was so angry with me for sullying the family name. He called me names, Thomas. Such horrible names. But I took it. I took it, so I could keep an eye out for my sister."

He knew she wasn't done, so he kept his mouth shut and let the flood of her trauma pour out of her.

"The boy's father… he… tried to force himself on me. I fought him and tore up his face pretty badly. He reported me to the sheriff and my father. I ran away, Thomas. I didn't know what else to do!"

"Rue," Thomas said softly.

In an instant, he knew the rest of the story. A whole series of little clues she'd given off, from her mannerisms to her reluctance to continue now snapped suddenly into place. He knew. But he let her tell it. She needed to say it, for her own sake.

"I ended up in the city. I tried to find work, but nobody would hire a seventeen-year-old girl with no family or home. I couldn't find work, or a place to stay. I slept on the street for weeks, begging for work, begging for scraps. Finally, I…"

Rue took a deep, steadying breath before she continued.

"I sold myself," she said, hiding her emotion behind a cold tone.

Thomas chuckled. He couldn't help it. She didn't see it. Her eyes snapped back up to his, fury raging in them.

"You think that's funny?" she snapped. He shook his head but was still smiling.

"No, that's not what's funny."

"Then please, share the joke with the rest of the class."

"You think I wouldn't want you because you've been used by other men," he stated simply.

Her glare told him in no uncertain terms he'd better explain, and fast, or she might hit him.

"Rue, do you love me?" he asked simply.

She frowned at him, the little furrow between her brows that always appeared when she frowned making its adorable appearance. He loved that furrow. Almost as much as he loved her smile. Clearly, she was unsure what that had to do with him laughing at her becoming a prostitute.

"It's a complicated emotion, but a simple question, Rue. Do you love me?" he asked again. After a long moment, she nodded.

"I do love you, Thomas. God help me, I do."

"I love you, too, Rue," he told her, amazed at how easy it was to say, once he'd gotten it out the first time. It just felt right.

"But what…" she trailed off.

"You love me, Rue. And I love you. Nothing else matters. At all. I wouldn't care even if you invented the profession yourself. It doesn't define you, Rue. You're not your past. If anyone knows that better than I do, I'd love to meet them." Thomas laughed and continued. "You're kind, generous, compassionate, bright, witty, playful, and have a fiery spirit. That's who you are. That's the woman I love."

"I'm afraid, Thomas," she admitted.

"Of what?" he asked.

"Of what people will do when the town finds out. And they will. You know they will sooner or later."

"Probably," Thomas agreed. "But if they can forgive my past?" He shook his head. "Believe me,

Rue, they won't have any trouble with yours."

"You really don't care?" she asked hesitantly, almost shyly, looking up at him from her lowered brows.

"Not in the least," Thomas agreed with a smile.

"You still want me?"

Thomas leaned down then, cupping her chin gently with one hand and raising her face to his.

His lips touched hers, then, and the rest of the world fell away.

He poured as much love, desire, tenderness, and promise into that kiss as he could. He felt all of that and more coming back to him through her.

Despite his focus on trying to convey to her just how much he did still want her, he lost himself in that kiss.

Thomas had no idea how long it lasted. It could have been ten seconds or ten days, he wouldn't have known the difference. When he pulled back, he drew in a long, slow breath.

She slowly opened her eyes, a tear slipping from each down her cheeks.

"Thomas," she said in something resembling awe. He smiled warmly at her.

"I know, a bit inappropriate, since I am still a priest, but I needed you to not just hear, but feel that I still want you. I'll behave myself from now on, until it's a more appropriate time."

Her smile held every bit of her. It was warm and sharp, it was playful and teasing, it was bright and now fully open.

"Please don't," she said simply.

Thomas just laughed and kissed her again.

Epilogue

"...and the deepest depths of fiery brimstone await!" thundered the preacher. His deep basso voice resonated dramatically in the chapel. The voice was at clear and hostile odds with the youthful, fresh-faced new preacher.

Thomas bit back a laugh. He looked over to Rue, sitting in the pew beside him, the whole row filled with Josie and the kids. All but the youngest had equally shocked, horrified expressions on their faces. He leaned over to Rue.

"Don't worry," he whispered. "I'll have a talk with him."

She turned her head enough to whisper back to him.

"For the love of God, please do!"

He'd have to, for the sake of the whole congregation. Thomas glanced back at Widow Riley. The look on her face almost made him laugh again.

It was a blend of shock, disgust, indignation, and irritation. She caught him looking her way and threw him a look that spoke volumes.

He could hear the words she couldn't say as clearly as if she'd spoken them.

"*This* is what you've abandoned us to?" that look said.

He smiled as apologetically as he could and turned front again. He'd talk with the new reverend. The people here didn't need to be scared to God, they needed to be loved to God. He'd seen that firsthand.

As the reverend wrapped up his incendiary sermon, the congregation stood. They seemed torn between wanting to stop and wait to greet the new reverend and wanting to escape to the freedom of the outdoors before they were swallowed by the gaping maw of the abyss that Reverend Bertrand seemed to think would open beneath the sinners among them at any moment.

Most chose the latter.

"Rever... I mean Mr. Jarrett?" a voice asked as he stepped out of the aisle to allow Rue and her family to exit. He looked down into the eyes of Annie Waterston.

"Why, Miss Annie! A delight to see you, as always," he said, to her obvious pleasure.

"Mama says I can invite you over for dinner again, if you like." She cast her eyes down bashfully, her tone hesitant and sweet.

He looked up to her parents, standing and watching nearby. Thomas dearly remembered Sam's words the day Jonathan had died, but he was still reluctant to presume everyone was comfortable with him, whatever they had said.

He needn't have worried. The Waterstons smiled at him with genuine warmth, and a little bit of amusement. He turned back to Annie.

"Miss Annie, I couldn't think of a single thing I'd like better. You just have your pa tell me when, and I'll be there with bells on."

Annie giggled, curtsied, and scampered back to her parents. He heard her hiss an excited whisper to them as she approached.

"He said yes!" she called back to him. Thomas chuckled, then heard a matching laugh from just behind him.

"Good afternoon, Mrs. Riley," he said as he turned with a smile.

Her own smile was perfectly charmed.

"Mr. Jarrett, you'd best watch yourself with that one," she chided lightly. "If you're not careful, Miss Briggs will have some fierce competition going for you."

Thomas grinned.

"Don't worry, Mrs. Riley. I'll let her down easy," he said.

"See that you do. Tragic enough you've broken this old woman's heart," she cackled. "I thought sure I'd lured you in with my cookies, but then that lovely Miss Briggs came to town and..." Mrs. Riley sighed a longsuffering sigh. "The better woman won, I'll admit."

"Mrs. Riley, you're incorrigible," he told her. She winked at him.

"Don't I know it. Say, as long as you're in the mood to be saying yes to dinner invitations, why don't you bring that sweet Miss Briggs along to my place Saturday evening."

"Ma'am, we'd be delighted, but I'm afraid I promised Miss Annie first for a date of her choosing. If she chooses Saturday…" he said, leaving the consequences of that choice hanging.

"Well, whatever day, then," she said dismissing his protest with a wave. "Not like I've got anything else going on. Just more confounded knitting with Mrs. Pomeroy."

Thomas chuckled at the tone in her voice.

"Here I thought you two were thick as thieves, just knitting up a happy little storm!"

"Well, it was quite all right the first few days, but it's been weeks, Mr. Jarrett! That old bird is driving me batty. You'd think we were already half in our graves, the way she goes on!"

Thomas laughed outright at that.

"Hang in there, Mrs. Riley. Me and the men will be by again tomorrow working on your new house. We'll have you moved into the new place by month's end."

"I sure hope so. It's mighty kind of you boys to come and build me a new house. I'd do it myself, you know, but my old hands don't last as long as they used to. Lord knows, I'd be dead before I finished!"

"Not a chance, Mrs. Riley. You'll outlive us all, I'm certain of it," Thomas said with a wink.

"Oh, tosh," she replied, but looked pleased by the remark. "Seriously, though, do bring Miss Briggs by for dinner this week. She's such a darling girl."

"She is that, Mrs. Riley," Thomas said, looking over to where Rue was helping wrangle the kids as she and Josie greeted the new reverend.

Rue looked up and caught his gaze. She smiled with a charmingly girlish bashfulness, and his grin broadened. He looked back to Widow Riley, who had a knowing look in her eye.

"I had a hunch about you two," she said. "I'm never wrong, you know. Not with my hunches."

"Not with your recipes, either," Thomas pointed out.

She laughed and swatted at his arm.

"Now you stop that, you charmer. You just let me know when you two will be by. I want to make a roast."

"Sounds delightful, Mrs. Riley. Thank you kindly for the invitation."

"My pleasure. And Mrs. Pomeroy's, she loves my roast." Mrs. Riley cackled again, patted his arm affectionately, and moved with her usual slow sureness exit.

She did not stop to greet the new reverend, Thomas noted.

He really did need to talk to the young man.

Thomas had had a rough time being accepted in town, too. Small towns were often a bit closed off to newcomers. Only Rue and Josie's unusual situation had allowed them to be welcomed in so easily.

He saw Rue, Josie, and the kids heading for the exit. Rue was giving him the "are you coming?" look. He nodded and moved to join her. He glanced the other way, toward the line waiting to speak to the new reverend. They'd talk later, he decided.

Plenty of time for that, he knew.

Rue took his hand as he fell into step beside her.

Such a simple gesture, he thought, but it said so much. He'd hold her hand until the day he died, if she'd let him.

Nothing had been settled, but they had both just sort of started operating under the premise that they were engaged already. Neither of them had proposed. It was possible neither of them ever would.

Or even needed to.

She could still change her mind, but by the smile she cast him at that moment, he doubted very much that would ever happen.

"We have a dinner engagement this week," he told her as they walked out into the wide, clear, blue sky.

"Oh?" she asked with a smile.

"With Mrs. Riley."

"That's wonderful," she said with a bright smile. "I adore that crazy old woman."

"Likewise," he said with a chuckle.

"I'll make an apple pie," she said.

Thomas stared in surprise.

"I didn't know you baked," he said. "And, I'll have you know, apple pie happens to be my absolute favorite."

"I know," she replied smugly. He blinked.

"How could you possibly know that?"

"I have my secrets, Mr. Jarrett."

"So it would seem," he replied with a determined grin. Someday, he'd know them all, he decided.

"What day?"

"Whatever day I'm not having dinner with the Waterstons," he told her.

"We've got two dinner engagements this week?" she asked in surprise.

"Actually, you weren't exactly invited to that one," he said, hedging a little. She laughed and gave him a playful shove. She didn't let go of his hand, though.

"You wouldn't have this problem if you'd quit flirting with all the pretty girls," she teased him.

"I'm absolutely going to tell Mrs. Riley you said that. She'll be plum tickled," Thomas laughed.

Rue made a face at him and he laughed harder.

"Oh, stop worrying," he told her playfully. "You know I belong to you."

"Do you?" she asked, pausing beside the wagon, looking up at him with a mostly serious expression.

"I do," he said, then leaned in and kissed her.

"Ew!" he heard a couple of the kids exclaim.

He drew back and made a face at them, then helped Rue into the back of the wagon.

With a quick handshake to the two older boys and a wave to the rest, he watched them as they rode down the road, heading back to their farm.

Rue watched him until they turned out of sight.

He would never in a million years have dreamed himself in the position he was now in. He was a respected member of a community that knew all about his past and had forgiven him his sins in an act of Christ-like mercy that deserved a place in the good book. He was helping out various members of the town with odd jobs while he got himself settled, and in the meantime, he was staying in Mr. Burley's spare room.

Someday, if he was lucky, he and Rue would be married in this very church, he thought. Then, he'd move in with her and the Briggses, and help them build a thriving farm. He didn't know a whole lot about farming beyond the basics, but he knew enough that with his strong hands, he'd be a valuable addition to the household.

But not today. Today, he'd go back to Mr. Burley's house and help rebuild a rocking chair and think about how many gifts had been given to a man like himself.

And, of course, say a prayer of gratitude, followed by one asking for nothing but wonderful things for the good people of this remarkable town.

The prayer of a Saint had to carry some weight, after all.

COMING SOON

Saint's Folly

THE SAINTS OF LAREDO

BOOK THREE

GRACE DONOVAN